Barbara Pym, who died in 1980, spent the last years of her life in an Oxfordshire village, sharing a small cottage with her sister. Between 1950 and 1961 she published six novels, all of which have now been reissued. In 1977, after a gap of sixteen years, she published *Quartet in Autumn*. It was treated as a major literary event, as was her next novel, *The Sweet Dove Died*. Three more novels, *A Few Green Leaves*, *An Unsuitable Attachment* and *An Academic Question* were published posthumously.

Hazel Holt was born in Birmingham in 1928 and educated at King Edward VI High School. On leaving Cambridge in 1950 she joined the staff of the International African Institute where she worked with Barbara Pym for over 25 years. As Barbara Pym's literary executrix she edited and prepared for press the typescripts of *An Unsuitable Attachment* and *An Academic Question*. She is married with one son and lives in London.

By the same author

Some Tame Gazelle
Excellent Women
Jane and Prudence
Less than Angels
A Glass of Blessings
No Fond Return of Love
Quartet in Autumn
The Sweet Dove Died
A Few Green Leaves
An Unsuitable Attachment
A Very Private Eye

BARBARA PYM

An Academic Question

GRAFTON BOOKS

A Division of the Collins Publishing Group

LONDON GLASGOW
TORONTO SYDNEY AUCKLAND

Grafton Books
A Division of the Collins Publishing Group
8 Grafton Street, London W1X 3LA

Special Overseas Edition 1987

First published in Great Britain by
Macmillan London Ltd 1986

ISBN 0-586-07365-5

Printed and bound in Great Britain by
Collins, Glasgow

Set in Bembo

NOTE

In 1970, still writing in spite of seven years of rejection, Barbara Pym began what she called her Academic Novel.

In June 1971 she wrote to Philip Larkin:

> Rather to my surprise I have nearly finished the first draft of another novel about a provincial university. . . . It was supposed to be a sort of Margaret Drabble effort but of course it hasn't turned out like that at all.

This draft, written in the first person, was, she felt, too 'cosy' to have any chance of being published in the unsympathetic literary climate of the day, so she wrote another version, this time in the third person, attempting to make the whole thing more 'sharp' and 'swinging'. But she was writing against the grain and was not happy with it and, although still 'tinkering with it' in October 1972, she became absorbed in the novel that was to become *Quartet in Autumn* and abandoned it.

In preparing this novel for publication I have amalgamated these two drafts, also making use of some notes that she made and consulting the original handwritten version, trying to 'smooth' them (to use Barbara's word) into a coherent whole. This version does, I hope, restore the Pym voice.

It is in many ways a transitional novel, as is its heroine, Caroline, by nature and upbringing an excellent woman, fitting uneasily into the more contemporary role of graduate wife.

Inspired by an academic wrangle in the journal *Africa*, it is very unlike her other books (though the reappearance of Sister Dew will delight readers familiar with her earlier novels) and therefore provides a fascinating addition to her published work.

When Barbara wrote this book (to which she never gave a title) she had no real expectation of its ever being published:

Perhaps my immediate circle of friends will like to read it.

It would please her very much to think that a wider circle of friends can read it now.

—HAZEL HOLT
Somerset, 1986

AN
ACADEMIC
QUESTION

I

'What jewels will you be wearing tonight, Mother?'

The question was typical of Coco and it was equally characteristic of Kitty Jeffreys that she should take it seriously.

'I'd thought of the topaz necklace,' she said, 'but perhaps it's a *little* too much . . . pearls might be better—the ones your father gave me when we were engaged.'

'Not your *black* pearls, then?' Coco sounded disappointed, excessively so for a man of forty-two. His mother at sixty-two was even better preserved and they made a handsome and interesting pair. I, at twenty-eight, felt old beside them, but then I had never had their self-absorption and passionate interest in what are usually regarded as trivialities.

'Pearls always look right,' I said politely, 'even artificial ones, though of course one can usually tell,' I added hastily, knowing that Kitty's were real. She had managed to bring away all her jewellery, as well as many financial assets, when she and her son had left their island in the Caribbean after the death of her husband and, more importantly, the election of an all-black government. It had seemed suitable at first, though now it was turning out to be less so, to return to the West Country town where Kitty had been born and where her sister still lived. Coco, with his degree from one of the more obscure American universities, had been awarded a research fellowship in Caribbean Studies at the university. The local residents were worried about the influx of West Indians into the town and money had been given for a study.

'I have to make *recommendations*,' Coco said, his long, useless fingers caressing the side of his glass. He now began to speculate on what he would wear for the party.

Polo shirts were out now, he said regretfully, for that style had admirably suited his tall, elegant figure. The high white polo collar had framed his thin, rather swarthy face like a cravat and this, with his dark curly hair carefully brushed forward, had given him something of the air of a Regency dandy.

'It's only a gathering of provincial academics,' I reminded him. 'Most of them will be wearing dark suits and clean shirts. Professor Maynard always gives this kind of party at the beginning of the autumn term. It's quite a tradition, but he's retiring next year, so I suppose this will be the last.'

Kitty pouted. She couldn't bear anything sad or coming to an end. She was said to have been a great beauty when, at eighteen, she had married the romantic stranger from the Caribbean over on a business trip. Even now she could look very pretty, though it was the prettiness of the twenties rather than the starker beauty of today. Coco had confided to me that she had sent her hair-piece to be styled at the best of the local hair-dressers. He asked, a little anxiously I thought, how I was going to do *my* hair.

'Oh, I'll just wash it,' I said defensively. 'Straight hair is best left as it is.'

'And yours always looks charming,' he said smoothly.

When I got home Inge, our Swedish au pair, and Kate, my four-year-old daughter, were sitting at the table in the kitchen having tea. Both of them, in name and appearance, seemed very suitable, I thought, for a modern couple like Alan and me, reading the *Guardian* and living in a rather new house with modern furniture that was beginning to look shabby. I suppose I should have been grateful for our relatively affluent lifestyle, made possible by a legacy from my grandmother, but going to see Kitty and Coco always made me dissatisfied with my surroundings. I looked around our red and white kitchen with distaste and wondered how I could ever have chosen the hideous washable wallpaper patterned with fruit and vegetables.

'Kate has been naughty,' said Inge smugly. She was a vast blonde girl, with huge limbs like a piece of modern sculpture. Kate was also on the solid side with blue eyes and Alan's reddish-gold hair.

I did not wait to hear the details of Kate's naughtiness but went upstairs to wash my hair. It was hanging dripping on my shoulders when Alan came in. I began to comb it and in doing so caught a strand of it on my cigarette. There was a smell of burning.

'Do you have to smoke all the time, Caro?' Alan said. 'I should've thought it would be inconvenient— not to mention lung cancer.'

And expense, I thought guiltily, while reminding Alan that he used to smoke once. I still didn't like him to criticise me. Naively I had imagined that he thought me perfect and it had been a shock when he began to find fault with me, even though it was only over un-important details.

We had first met at a university which, to my moth-er's grief, was neither Oxford nor Cambridge, and had fallen in love when I was slightly on the rebound from a Byronic-looking cad with political ambitions. Alan's dusty fair eyelashes, grey eyes and slight but fascinating provincial accent had attracted me. He had seemed to be the kind of person who would cherish and look after me and up to a point he was and still is.

I had been christened Caroline, which in my teens I had changed to Caro because of poor Lady Caroline Lamb, who said she was like the wreck of a little boat for she never came up to the sublime and beautiful. At sixteen it had seemed touching and amusing to think of oneself in this way, but as I grew older I could see that it was less admirable. After the misery of the Byronic affair, which had been the inevitable result of this early foolishness, I had tried to forget the Caro side of me, though the name still stuck.

Fiction, journalism and the conversation of other university wives, some of whom had part-time jobs, tended to make me see myself as a frustrated graduate wife, though I had married straight from university and had never had anything that might be considered as a proper job, nor was there any particular career that I wanted to follow. I was, however, conscious of lacking any special maternal feeling and this seemed an even greater inadequacy. I loved Kate and worried about her very often, but Inge was so much better with her than I was. Still, I felt proud that I had produced a child, though disappointed that I did not feel more 'fulfilled'.

'Is your hair going to be dry in time?' Alan asked.

'Of course! You don't think I'd go to the Maynards' with wet hair, do you?'

'I never quite know.'

'I've put out a clean shirt for you,' I said. 'Will you be wearing your grey suit?'

'Yes, I suppose so,' he said without interest, so different from Coco. 'I'd like a cup of tea.'

'Inge will make you one when she's finished with Kate.' Alan's liking for cups of tea at all hours had been an endearing trait which now irritated me. Of course he had developed a taste for more sophisticated and suitable drinks, but the love of tea remained.

'Inge doesn't know how to make tea properly. I'll do it myself.'

I did not offer to do it—Alan was as domesticated as I was.

I stood at the open window rubbing my wet hair with a towel. We lived in the higher part of the town and I could see the large old Victorian houses down the hill, some of which were now private hotels, filled with retired people who had settled here because of the mild climate. The town had been a spa in the eighteenth century but nobody came to drink the waters now and the pump room was a sad, deserted building, the subject of letters in the local paper which periodically demanded that something be 'done' with it. The university had grown up from the local technical college and was regarded with dislike and increasing fear and suspicion by the local residents. This summer the students had rioted, though mildly compared with others who appeared to have more worthy grievances. Ours concerned themselves with trivia, ranging from the provision of slot machines for contraceptives to complaints about the food.

Our house was only neo-Georgian, the genuine ones being occupied by people like Crispin Maynard, the head of Alan's department, whose party we were going to this evening. Only a few days ago Crispin and his wife Margaret had returned from their villa in Italy. I had watched them unloading the luggage from their car while Alan remarked scornfully on the ridiculous anachronism of a professor at a provincial university having a villa in Italy, just like something out of Trollope.

'I know,' I had said, 'but in a way that's what one likes about him. While the students were rioting Crispin was already on his way to Lake Garda.'

There was nothing to be ashamed of in having inherited a villa from his family, and it made me glad to realise that not everyone was being whittled down to the same size, as Alan and some of his colleagues would have wished. I had wanted it myself once, but now it seemed dreary. Perhaps that was why I liked Coco and Kitty.

I looked in on Kate before we went out. One sometimes reads in Edwardian memoirs of a child retaining a romantic memory of its mother dressed to go out to a party, coming in to say good night. I wondered how Kate would remember me in my trouser suit which gave little scope for conventional glamour. Perhaps, years hence, a certain scent would bring back the occasion, for the bottle had upset and I was stupefied by the expensive aura.

'Is that the scent I gave you last Christmas?' Alan asked and seemed pleased when I confirmed that it was.

'Unfortunately I spilt it, so it may overpower everybody.'

Alan smiled, as if that would add to his prestige in some way.

'In we go,' said Alan, as we went through the open door into the Maynards' hall, perfectly furnished with all the right kind of things.

Margaret Maynard was waiting to greet her guests with a suitable word for each one. She was a tall, splendid woman with red-gold hair, wearing a green pre-Raphaelite kind of dress which now looked surprisingly up-to-date. She had two sons, two daughters and several grandchildren. She was an excellent housekeeper and cook and did all her husband's typing, this last skill dating from the days when it was regarded as one of the duties of an academic wife. Alan did his own typing and this seemed to cut me off from his work. I did not have the opportunity to suggest an apt phrase or rectify a misplaced footnote—there would be no fulsome acknowledgement of my assistance when Alan published his first book.

Crispin Maynard was in every way as splendid as his wife. Also tall, with white hair, he was in his mid-sixties, with old-fashioned, courteous manners.

'My dear, how charming you look! Let me get you something to eat and drink.'

The food at the Maynards' parties was always good and there was plenty of it so that one didn't have to have supper first. I took a small pizza and stood with it in my hand, hoping to be able to take a bite before anybody came to talk to me. Alan had gone off to talk academic shop with a fellow lecturer and I found myself having to fall back, temporarily I hoped, on Heather Armitage, the wife of the assistant librarian, an anxious-looking woman in her late thirties who seemed never to have recovered from the worries of card indexes and bibliographies in the days when she too had worked in a library and, I presumed, snared George Armitage. Her hair was cut short in one of the fashionable styles of the moment, which exposed her face and neck mercilessly.

Heather had a part-time job in the university library but that, apparently, was not stimulating enough for a graduate wife and she was going on about how she was helping someone with some research, 'not one's own,' she added apologetically, 'but very worthwhile really.'

My eyes were free to rove around the room while I listened, for Heather was one of those people who do not expect their own experiences to be met with an account of one's own. Who does when one comes to think of it? We all like to hold the floor even if we have nothing of general or universal interest to say. I noticed Dr. Cranton, the head librarian, discoursing to a small captive circle, but I could not guess at what he might be saying. His wife was quietly eating in a corner. Two young lecturers, man and woman, were eyeing each other with love or even lust, though I could not help noticing that the girl's left hand was absently toying with a small vol-au-vent as if impatient for the opportunity to carry it to her mouth. On the whole they were a rather dull lot of people and Coco and his mother had not yet arrived. They always made a point of arriving last at everything, like royalty. It was said that they had to rest for at least two hours before a party and it was certainly true that Coco was always 'preserving' himself in the way that Kitty had obviously done all her life.

'Here comes Coco,' said Heather suddenly, 'last as usual. Such a silly name!'

'He was christened Corcoran,' I explained, 'and that's a bit much.'

'Very fashionably dressed, isn't he?' said Heather critically. 'I suppose that's quite the latest.'

'Obviously, if Coco's wearing it,' I said. Evidently a life spent with card indexes did not make for generosity of spirit, I thought. 'Don't you think he looks distinguished?'

'Has he got coloured blood, do you suppose? That very curly hair . . . I've always wondered.'

'His father was white, but the family has been settled on the island for many generations, so perhaps way back . . .'

'Of course the races should mix,' said Heather stoutly. 'I'm all in favour of that.'

Kitty *was* wearing her black pearls after all. They certainly looked good with her grey dress.

Coco greeted us. 'You look charming, both of you. Were you having a nice catty girls' conversation?'

'Certainly not,' said Heather indignantly.

'We were saying how distinguished you looked,' I said with slight malice.

Heather looked annoyed. 'I must go and find George,' she said.

We watched her go over to a group that included her husband and some grey-looking sociologists and drag him away to talk to the librarian's wife.

'And must you go and find Alan?' Coco asked.

'No—I'll leave him to find me if he wants to.'

'Perhaps he doesn't at the moment,' Coco remarked, with a glance towards Alan, who was talking to a rather striking-looking youngish woman whom I didn't remember seeing before.

'Who's that?' I asked.

'Oh, somebody new—Iris something,' said Coco indifferently.

'She's attractive, isn't she?'

'If you like that sort of thing. Do you mind not being beautiful?'

'Of course not. One doesn't expect to be *beautiful*. And anyway, I'm not hideous,' I felt bound to point out.

'No, you have quite an intriguing face. Your eyes are good but your nose is too long. You could have it altered.'

'Oh, don't be ridiculous.' This was a conversation Coco and I quite often had, but it seemed frivolous and out of place in this kind of academic gathering.

'I think Mother feels the loss of her beauty,' Coco went on. 'Not the *loss* exactly, because she'll always be a beautiful woman.'

'But one loses the freshness of youth,' I suggested.

'Yes—but youth is boring, after all.'

'Usually it is only the young who think so,' I pointed out. 'How does Kitty manage to be so splendid anyway?'

'Oh, loving beautiful objects and surrounding oneself with them. Look at her now!'

We joined Kitty and Crispin Maynard, who were examining a small marble head that he had evidently brought back from Italy.

'Oh, I just *love* it!' Kitty said.

'Then you must have it.' Crispin presented it to her with a bow.

'Goodness knows where we'll put it,' Coco whispered to me. 'Mother just *collects* objets d'art!'

'I know,' I murmured, remembering the elegant clutter—there was no other word for it—in the Jeffreys' flat. I was beginning to feel tired, and the obligation to admire both Coco and Kitty was beginning to exhaust me as it usually did after a while.

I looked for Alan to suggest that we might go home and found him in Crispin's study, not talking to anyone, just standing with a glass in his hand, looking rather annoyed. There was no sign of the woman he had been talking to earlier. Crispin was sitting at his desk, surrounded by graduate students, including several Africans.

'What's happening?' I asked Alan.

'Crispin's distributing largesse,' said Alan dryly.

'Offprints of his last article, you mean? The one everyone said was so good?'

'*Good . . .*'

I realised that the adjective I had chosen was much too simple, much too loaded with other, more ancient meanings to describe what the article might have been. I should have said 'able', 'provocative', 'controversial', 'sound'.

'Professor Maynard has taught us so much of our history,' said one of the Africans, 'that we didn't know before.'

'A lot of English people don't know their own history,' I suggested.

'But that's hardly the same thing.' The cold, rather sarcastic voice was that of Dr. Cranton, the librarian. I knew it wasn't really the same thing, just as I knew that Crispin Maynard had been a pioneer in the field of the history of pre-literate peoples, 'making it up', as I saw it, from oral traditions and manuscript material. This was Alan's subject, too, but he had come to it from anthropology whereas Crispin had started out as a historian. It seemed not unlikely that they would be rivals in the same field, as academics so often are, although the gap in their ages and outlook was great.

'He *is* generous,' I said as we walked home. 'He gave Kitty Jeffreys a marble bust.'

'I wish you wouldn't spend so much time with Coco, darling,' Alan said. 'You seemed to be talking to him all evening.'

'Well, I was jealous of you, too, talking to that dark girl!'

'You mean Iris Horniblow? She's new in the department. But I didn't mean that *I* was jealous of Coco in that way.'

'No, you wouldn't be when you know there's no reason.'

'I can't think what you see in him.'

'I feel at ease with him. He's like . . .'

'A sister to you?' Alan suggested.

'In a way.' I didn't say that I found him much more sympathetic and amusing than my own sister. 'Let's say Coco's a sort of brother. Anyway, I was talking to lots of other people as well—Heather for one.'

'You didn't say a word to Evan Cranton, though.'

'You know I'm frightened of him.'

'Frightened of the librarian—Caro, *really*!'

'I don't know what to talk to him about and he doesn't help one at all—I don't even know what his interests are.'

Alan paused for a moment. 'Well, Anglican-Methodist reunion, for one thing, and entomology, oh, and

manuscript Africana, of course—you know he's building a collection here.'

'I didn't, actually, but I suppose I could have talked
about insects in a simple way.'

'Of course—any intelligent girl should find plenty
to talk about there. You don't *try*. And if you are going
to get yourself a part-time job you may well find yourself coming into contact with him.'

'But I don't want *that* kind of job, I don't want to
be like Heather, writing things on cards and putting
them in boxes. I thought I might help Dolly in her shop.'

'Caro, you can't work in a junk shop—that really
isn't good enough.'

I was too tired to protest that Dolly really kept a
sort of second-hand book shop, even if she did have a
few 'objects' on a table outside when it was fine. We
had reached home and I went upstairs and fell into bed,
hoping that Alan would follow me. But instead he went
into his study, saying that he would do a bit more to
the article he was writing. I lay listening to the tapping
of his typewriter, but soon sleep overcame me and the
next thing I was conscious of was Kate's enthusiastic
greeting far too early in the morning.

II

It was hard to believe that Dolly Arborfield was Kitty Jeffreys' sister, though one could detect a slight family resemblance in features. Dolly's hair was grey and frizzy and she wore clothes that melted into her background of old books, junk and animals. She was some years older than Kitty and would often joke about her name, Dorothea, meaning 'gift of God'. To her parents, who had wanted a son but were only to have daughters, the name may have had a certain irony, especially as Dolly wasn't even the pretty one. 'Gift of God I was not,' she would say, 'but they weren't to know it at the time.' It was Kitty who had made the brilliant, or at least wealthy, marriage. Dolly had remained single, though she had always given me to understand that her life had not been without love. But now, in her sixties, she had grown away from human beings and only kept in touch with her former lovers for practical and material advantages; she was more moved by the sight of a hedgehog's little leg raised to scratch itself than by any memory of a past love. These same hedgehogs were one of the reasons why Dolly never went away. The habit of staying at home had its origin, she told me, in a quarrel with a neighbour who had refused to put out food for the hedgehogs during Dolly's absence. That neighbour had long since died and another, more accommodating, had taken her place but now it was too late, for with age Dolly had lost the desire for a change of scene. 'Wherever you go, you take yourself with you,' she said, 'and that is too upsetting in beautiful surroundings.'

Alan thought I saw too much of Dolly as I did of Coco and his mother, but whereas he despised them, he was a little afraid of Dolly. He mistrusted her preoccupation with animals and her interest in the problems of loneliness, while her sardonic attitude towards academics and particularly those in the new universities made him uneasy in her presence. He also thought that she was a bad influence on me because she was always smoking.

When I went to see her the day after the party she was sitting up in bed counting her cigarette coupons and arranging them in bundles of five hundred.

'I'm going to get a casserole on a stand,' she announced, 'with a little night light burning underneath to keep things hot.'

'But would you ever use it?' I asked doubtfully.

'I *might*! But if I don't I can give it to somebody for Christmas.'

I sat down on the edge of the bed and looked through the catalogue of 'gifts' with her. The coloured illustrations showed men doing so many manly things with garden tools and power drills and cars that I realised that I should have been saving up to get something for Alan instead of smoking a brand that did not offer coupons. Then I turned over the page and came upon a bathroom filled with beautiful towels, a kitchen bright with new saucepans and a group of well-groomed people drinking sherry out of cut-crystal glasses.

'Oh, dear,' I sighed, 'it's all so unlike *my* home.'

Outside it was raining, which was probably why Dolly was not yet up. She stayed in bed, usually, because she found it convenient to do such things as sorting out her coupons, reading and writing letters there. It was very different from the careful resting and preserving of themselves indulged in by Kitty and Coco. In fine weather, Dolly would be up at dawn observing nature in her garden, drinking coffee, smoking and doing housework. Her unpredictability was one of the things I liked about her.

I began to tell her about the Maynards' party and described what people looked like and what we had to eat, though the latter interested her more than the former.

'Alan thinks I ought to have a job,' I told her, 'and as I can't really help him with his work I suppose I'll have to look for something else—something to do with research and card indexes he would like, but I'd prefer something unusual that I could make my own.'

'What about the old people's home?' Dolly suggested.

My dismay must have shown itself on my face, for

she went on to say that some of the people there were quite interesting.

'It's for gentlefolk, as Sister Dew never tires of pointing out, and most of them have their own furniture with them.'

The idea of elderly persons of gentle birth surrounded by their own bits of Chippendale and Sheraton, not to mention Chelsea, Waterford and Meissen, was not one that attracted me and I said so.

'Besides, what could I do there?'

'Read to them,' said Dolly.

'*Read* to them? How appalling! What should I read?'

'Novels and biographies, poetry, the Bible—do you know that Professor Maynard sometimes looks in on a retired missionary there?'

'Crispin Maynard? Still, he's a kind man—it's the sort of thing he would do. And wasn't he at an African university once? They'd have that in common, perhaps. I suppose I *could* read to the old people if they really needed someone. I'll think it over and let you know, and now I must go home.'

'I rather wondered how you could spare the time to visit me on a Sunday morning,' Dolly remarked.

'I've done a casserole for today,' I explained.

'I should have thought Alan was the sort who would have demanded roast beef and Yorkshire pudding on a Sunday.'

Indeed he did and that very characteristic was one of the things that had seemed so attractive about him when we first met. But now I was trying to make him more adventurous about food, though I did not reveal this to Dolly.

On the way home I passed the parish church. The

congregation was just coming out from the morning service. Through the open door I could hear the sound of the organ, rich, sugary, almost treacly, the harmonies having an old-fashioned air with echoes of the Victorian age of church music in them. This was perhaps not surprising since the organist was Coco. He and Kitty, so they told me, had been pillars of the Anglican church, St. Michael's, Paradise Bay, and his style of playing belonged to that paternalistic society which had now vanished. Even here, though, there were one or two black faces in the congregation and as I passed the lych-gate I could see Kitty, her head graciously inclined as it must so often have been on the island, in conversation with one of them, an elderly woman in a hat that almost rivalled her own.

I could not wait to see Kitty or Coco and knew that I was late when I arrived home and found Inge getting ready to go out. On Sundays she usually went to a Scandinavian club in the town which I called the Seamen's Mission after something I remembered in Ibsen, though Alan did not think it a very amusing joke. I supposed that the girls met together to complain about their employers, but I felt smug because we made a point of having lunch uncomfortably early on Sundays so that she could get away in good time.

'Potatoes are cooked already,' she greeted me re-proachfully.

'Well,' I said, going into the study, 'I thought you were waiting for lunch.'

'I'm waiting for Inge to stop glowering over me,' Alan said, 'I wish you'd organise her a bit better. Can't we even have a glass of sherry?'

'Yes, let's. I'll tell her to have her lunch and go.

Then we can have a civilised meal—if anything can be called that with Kate around.'

'At least we'll be free of Inge's brooding presence.'

Over lunch I told him about the old people's home and Dolly's suggestion that I should read to them. Rather to my surprise he did not express immediate disapproval, but old people were rather in fashion at the time. Every week one or other of the quality Sunday papers included a feature on the elderly, and if it could be shown that they were being ill-treated or neglected so much the better.

'Crispin Maynard goes there,' I said, 'to visit some old missionary. And Dolly tells me they're all gentlefolk.'

'You make it sound just the kind of thing your mother would approve of,' said Alan ironically, and I saw what he meant. My mother, living in a picturesque cottage in an Oxfordshire village, had still not accepted Alan as a husband for me. There was something not quite right, not exactly what one would have wished for, about an academic post at a new university that had once been a technical college. My sister had also been a disappointment to her, for she was living in London with a television designer and there seemed no likelihood that they would ever get married.

'This missionary that Crispin goes to visit—could you find out his name?'

'Yes, of course,' I said, surprised. 'Could it be somebody you know?'

'Not in that way. But it might be somebody I know *of*,' said Alan thoughtfully. 'Somebody of considerable interest to Crispin and to me.'

III

The next morning, just after Alan had gone off to his department, the front door bell rang. From a side window I could see a female figure in long black robes standing on the doorstep. A nun collecting for something, I thought, reaching for my purse to find the silver coin that superstition demanded, just like crossing a Gypsy's palm, but when I opened the door I realised that it was one of Alan's girl students wearing a black floor-length coat. She asked if she could see me for a minute.

I invited her in, thinking that this was perhaps the opportunity I had been waiting for. My husband's students ought to bring their problems to me, I felt, preparing myself to give advice on some personal problem—

contraception, even abortion. But my hopes were dashed when she said, 'Oh, Mrs. Grimstone, I wonder if I could borrow your sewing machine?'

I now saw that she had a flowered carrier bag with her from which she took out a long evening dress in the style of the 1930s, which probably came from one of Dolly Arborfield's jumble sales in aid of animal charities. The girl wanted to alter it to fit herself for a college dance, she explained.

I left her with the machine, feeling slightly let down and not a little resentful, for Alan thought it unsuitable that I should wear jumble-sale clothes as the students did.

I had agreed to go to the old people's home with Dolly that afternoon and I looked forward to the ordeal—experience—privilege—with mixed feelings. I saw again the *Sunday Times* colour supplement and the pictures of the old people, their faces fashionably out of focus, as they must have sat staring hopelessly at the interviewer and his smart photographer. But these people I was going to see would not be like that. There would be fewer of them, they would be well cared for, they would not have been abandoned by their relatives. All the same, how did I know that I was going to be any good with them? Even reading aloud, which had seemed simple enough, now appeared to be beyond me. They might even be deaf.

My first sight of the home reassured me a little. It was called Normanhurst, a large Edwardian detached house with a gravel drive and a lot of evergreen shrubs clustering around the front door. It was a fine day and round the side of the house I could see elderly people walking slowly in the garden, or 'grounds' as Sister Dew preferred to call them. Perhaps they would all be outside,

I thought hopefully, and not in a position to be read to.

Sister Dew was at the door to greet us and Dolly introduced me.

'A young face,' said Sister Dew brightly. 'That's what they like to see!'

I, who had been feeling at my most dire, hung my head in embarrassment, but I supposed that the face of a not particularly pretty woman of twenty-eight must seem young to people in their seventies and eighties.

Sister Dew's appearance bore out the brightness of her tone. She had a smooth, well-made-up face, shining blue tip-tilted glasses, short grey hair and good regular false teeth with pale pink gums. She must have inspired confidence in most of her charges, if that was how they were to be regarded; only a few might have felt despair.

'Reverend Stillingfleet is all ready for you, dear,' she said, indicating a room on the ground floor.

'*Mister* Stillingfleet, unless he prefers to be called Father,' Dolly muttered, clenching her fists, a characteristic gesture she had when annoyed.

She had tapped on the door and we walked in together. I saw immediately what Dolly had meant when she told me that the inhabitants of Normanhurst were allowed to have their own 'things'. Mr. Stillingfleet's were carved wooden stools, masks, statues, rough wooden implements, presumably African, and coloured hangings that Sister Dew probably considered unhygienic. It said something for her that she had not forbidden them, but I had no doubt that they were often taken down and given a good beating or shaking in the garden.

A fragile old man with light watery eyes was sitting up in bed. Dolly addressed him, speaking clearly and rather roughly without any kind of condescension or allowance for his age and fragility.

'This is Mrs. Grimstone who has come to read to you,' she said. 'Her husband is a lecturer at the university and she will read anything you ask her to.'

Mr. Stillingfleet smiled. He looked less alarmingly old when he did this and I judged him to be at least eighty.

'I'm nearly blind, my dear,' he explained. 'But I can still hear quite well.'

Dolly gave a satisfied nod and went briskly away.

Mr. Stillingfleet reached out his hand.

'If you would not mind taking that journal which I asked Sister Dew to put on top of the box—that one, with the terracotta cover . . .'

I looked at the place indicated, a large box or chest secured with a broad strap. As he said, there was a pile of miscellaneous books and journals, and the terra cotta one was on top. I picked it up and to my surprise saw that it was one that Alan took—in fact, I believed that the article he was working on was intended for it. This seemed an odd coincidence until I remembered Alan asking me to find out the old missionary's name. Presumably he knew of him already in connection with some aspect of his work. I was even more surprised when the old man asked me to read an article by Crispin Maynard. At first I stumbled over the unfamiliar terminology, but after a while I remembered the days when I first knew Alan and had tried to keep up with his work, and the words came more easily. At one point Mr. Stillingfleet stopped me and asked if there was a footnote at that point. I saw that there was and he asked me to read it out. There was a reference to an article of his

own, published in 1913. He smiled and nodded as I
pronounced his name and the title of the article. I thought
this rather touching, an old man's pride in a past achieve-
ment, even if it had been no more than a ten-page article
in an obscure missionary journal. I wondered if Alan
would be interested.

Just as I had finished reading the article, Sister Dew
came into the room bearing a cup of Bovril on a tray.

'Now we mustn't over-tire ourselves, must we?'
she said, perhaps including me with her patient, and
certainly my throat was dry with the effort of reading.

Mr. Stillingfleet thanked me and prepared to take
his Bovril. I put the journal back on top of the box and
followed Sister Dew out of the room, feeling rather
pleased with myself.

'You were a success all right,' she said. 'I could tell
that. Such funny things he wants read to him, but with
your hubby at the university I expect you're used to it.
Now what about a cup of tea before you go? I'm sure
you've earned it.'

I accepted the tea gratefully, though normally I would
not have chosen it at that time of day. As I drank it
Sister Dew chattered on about Mr. Stillingfleet—how
he'd been married but his wife had died 'in the mission
field', as she put it, and then he had come to live with
his sister in a village nearby, then *she'd* died and he hadn't
been able to cope on his own, so he'd come here to
Normanhurst, to end his days surrounded by his treasures.

'Treasures?' I queried. 'You mean those carvings
and things he has in his room?'

'Yes, his toys, really,' said Sister Dew indulgently.
'That's how I think of them. But of course it's the things
in the box that he values most—manuscripts and that.'

'Oh, I see, notes and that kind of thing, I suppose.'

'Yes. He wouldn't let the Professor look in there when he came to see him.'

I supposed she must mean Crispin Maynard.

'They couldn't be *valuable*,' Sister Dew said doubtfully. 'I mean not to anyone but the Reverend Stillingfleet, could they? But he was quite firm about it. He said to me, "I don't want anyone tampering with my box." Those were his very words!'

'I suppose old people get like that,' I said, and of course one could see how they would. Alan didn't like it if I moved anything in his study. I sometimes felt that he looked on me as a meddling, ignorant servant who might use a valuable manuscript for lighting the fire.

'Old Mr. Stillingfleet's got a box of papers,' I said to Alan, 'and not even Crispin Maynard is allowed to *tamper* with them.'

'Do try and have a look at them some time,' said Alan casually. 'Who knows, the unexpurgated version of his *Tales Told by the Black Washeli* might be there.'

'What's that—a piece of pornographic literature?'

'Don't be silly, Caro. It's just what it says—the full, uncut version of old Stillingfleet's book published in 1920. Both Crispin and I have been trying for ages to get a look at it. Of course he didn't tell me about Stillingfleet being here—he wouldn't, naturally. Now it's up to you, Caro, to get a look at it.'

I laughed at the idea of myself trying to extricate the manuscript from the wooden box, though it would be nice if I could do something to please Alan.

IV

I continued to go regularly to Normanhurst. My reading improved and I no longer stumbled over unfamiliar words; Mr. Stillingfleet and I became almost friendly in a curious way. Yet I got no nearer to seeing the contents of the box. I was not even allowed to touch it. The books and articles I was asked to read were always put out ready so that there was never any need to look for anything. I had to be content with the feeling that I was 'doing good' to an old person and this was certainly satisfying to me, who had never consciously done good to anybody. And yet it was not quite enough and I began to get bored and impatient for something to happen. Alan stopped asking me about the unpublished manuscript but I knew he was working on his article. The tapping of his typewriter kept him from coming up to bed and I felt abandoned and neglected. Coco, in whom I had unwisely confided one evening when he took me out for a drink, advised me to acquire a lover.

'That's what people do,' he said, as if I had no knowledge of the world.

'Yes, of course,' I agreed. 'But who, or *whom*, come to that—who *is* there in a place like this?'

Coco became vague. He had nobody definite in mind and I certainly wouldn't be satisfied with just anybody. A distinguished artist or writer, even a member of a noble family or an exiled royal—perhaps there was one such living in the town. After all, it was the kind of place people like that come to—witness the example of himself and his mother.

'But an exiled royal would probably be decayed and moth-eaten,' I protested, 'and I want better than that.'

'A pity,' Coco sighed. 'It would have been amusing—I should have liked acting as a go-between.'

I was remembering this conversation one morning when I had arranged to meet Alan for lunch at the university. But the new clean functional senior common room and refectory which had arisen so surprisingly, tacked on to the nineteenth-century building that had housed the old technical college, did not seem to have the atmosphere for any kind of love affair, certainly not for anything as old-fashioned as a romance of the kind Coco wanted for me. There should be no malice or evil here either, I thought, as I waited for Alan to come out of his lecture. These buildings must surely provide the setting for a fresh start where the old intrigues and petty academic irritations could be forgotten.

The people around me seemed an ordinary enough lot of men, perhaps a little rougher and less sophisticated than, say, a group of television people whom I had occasionally met with my sister who lived in London. I knew them to be lecturers in English literature, history, languages, anthropology, sociology and economics. But how many of them were also good husbands and wonderful lovers, tender fathers and dutiful sons, I wondered. Precious few of them could be all these things, of course. I saw Alan as an adequate husband, an unenthusiastic lover, a dutiful father and a son who despised the family he had grown beyond. But he was said to be brilliant at his work and a great help to his students. Also, and even more important, I had once been in love with him and in a way I still was. But waiting here, without drink inside me, conscious of people around me who appeared not to be conscious of me, I tried to step outside myself. Carefully, cautiously, with a cool eye and as much detachment as I could muster, I peeped at myself and Alan, as it were lifting the corner of a curtain or peering through a chink in a lighted window. I saw two people, together yet apart, not exactly incompatible, and I wondered if it was my fault.

'Oh, *there* you are, Caro.' Alan couldn't help sounding a little irritable, as if I was to blame for his being late.

'Didn't anybody get you a drink?'

'No, but it doesn't matter. I've been all right here.'

He got the drinks and we sat together in silence. Some of Alan's colleagues were already eating, refuelling at the trough, to enable them the better to support what most of them regarded as a 'crushing teaching load' which could amount to as much as eight or ten hours a week. Most of them nodded to Alan as they came in but nobody joined us; each person was intent on his or her own business; there was nothing social about the occasion. Most of the young lecturers, except for the very junior ones, were at the stage of feeling dissatisfied with their positions. Alan himself—*Dr.* Alan Grimstone, for he was, of course, a Ph.D.—had been feeling for some time that he ought to be moving onwards and upwards. Just as our green Triumph Herald was no longer quite big enough, so the position of lecturer did not give him all the scope he needed. He knew that he was looked on as able and promising, but he was like a card in a game of patience, his moves blocked by cards of a higher suit. The one most in his way was Crispin Maynard and, although Alan could not, of course, hope to get his chair when he retired, he felt that once Crispin had gone, his own upward path to progress would be easier. My mother, much addicted to games of patience (Alan's mother never had time), would so often wail in a despairing tone, 'But I can't get the two—there's a Black King in the way!', which exactly expressed Alan's feelings.

In the meantime, while waiting for Crispin to be removed by the natural process of retirement, Alan had entered into the field of academic rivalry in learned journals and the article he was working on now was likely to challenge Crispin's supremacy in his own field.

Alan went up to the bar to get us another drink. As he did so a woman waylaid him.

'How *does* one refer to that sort of thing in a footnote?' I heard her say. 'I mean, the report's unpublished and one shouldn't really have had access to it at all. . . .'

'I don't know if you've met my wife?' Alan brought her over, introducing her as Dr. Iris Horniblow, who had joined the department this term. It was the person

Alan had been talking to at the Maynards' party. She was striking to look at, with thick, square-cut dark hair and bold brown eyes. I noticed that she wore a very wide gold wedding ring.

'Well, not exactly.' Dr. Horniblow acknowledged me with a nod. 'I think I've seen you with your little girl.'

That seemed to put me in my place. I wondered if she had any children and was not surprised to learn that she had two, a boy and a girl, named Luke and Alice. I felt a little scornful when I heard the names, though my own Kate was not much better.

Dr. Horniblow said something about sex-education programmes and asked if I thought they were a good thing. I had no ready answer but said rather feebly that perhaps people like us were meant to do that kind of teaching ourselves, at home.

'At the mother's knee,' said Dr. Horniblow—I could not think of her as Iris—in a tone that poured scorn on such an old-fashioned notion. 'That could give rise to serious psychological difficulties—on the other hand, one doesn't want them to pick up wrong ideas from other children.'

'Or from animals,' said Alan.

I knew he was thinking of the time when Kate, after a visit to Dolly, had come home chattering about the baby hedgehogs and how the mummy hedgehog had found them in the leaves early one morning. Did she not show any curiosity as to how they got there in the first place? he asked me insistently. No, she hadn't, and, when later I had tried to explain to her something about the babies coming out of the mummy hedgehog's tummy, I knew it was not good enough and that Alan would be displeased to think of Kate learning about such things from Dolly and from such a low form of life as the hedgehog, which was covered with fleas.

'Oh, cats and dogs can be quite useful,' said Dr. Horniblow. 'Not neutered cats, of course,' she added. 'A neutered cat is no good to man or beast.' She laughed and left us to have lunch.

'What a horrid thing to say,' I protested.

'What?'

'About a neutered cat.'

'*Really*, darling . . . Iris is a great asset to the department, as a matter of fact. She's very able.'

This last was high praise, as I knew, and I could hardly argue against it.

'We must ask her in some time,' I suggested, trying to please, 'with her husband, of course. What does he do?'

'I haven't the faintest idea. They're divorced, actually.'

'Oh. Did she drive him away or did he just abandon her?'

'I don't know the details. There are other reasons for a marriage breaking up,' said Alan, with the serious, frowning look on his face that I always loved. 'I should think she's had a pretty tough time.'

'Yes, maybe she has,' I said, trying to see her in this light. Her rather unpleasantly aggressive manner might be putting a brave face on things, then—might conceal all kinds of uncertainty and unhappiness.

'What did you advise her to do about the footnote?'

'What footnote?'

'The one citing unpublished material that she wasn't really supposed to have seen.'

'Oh, *that.*' Alan smiled what I can only describe as an enigmatic smile, but I never heard the answer because Coco came up to the table at that moment and asked if he could join us.

Alan was polite but distant. Like most of his colleagues he was suspicious of Coco, particularly in the academic sense. What exactly did the research fellow in Caribbean Studies *do*, apart from hobnobbing with the West Indian factory workers and bus drivers in a pub in the town? Ought he not to have published, or be in the act of getting published, or even 'preparing for publication'—that vague, useful phrase—some monograph, report or article on some aspect of his work?

'*Such* a morning!' Coco went through the motions of being utterly exhausted.

'How is your fieldwork going, then?' Alan asked, rather meanly, I thought.

'Oh, that's all right. I got one of my informants to distribute copies of a questionnaire I thought up and that will keep them happy for weeks. Fifty questions to be answered.'

'And then you'll prepare the data for computerisation, I suppose,' Alan said.

'Oh, yes—whatever it is that people do.' Coco waved his hand languidly. 'All those pretty little girls in white overalls.'

'Won't you join us for lunch?' I asked.

'No, Caro dear. Some relatives descended on us—from my father's side. Quite black. Such a shock for Mother, of course. We hardly even *knew* about them.'

'I suppose there always has been a good deal of intermarriage in the islands—it's only what one would expect,' Alan said.

'Of course. There has been and it *is* only what one would expect—but when they turn up on the doorstep . . .'

'Poor Kitty,' I murmured. 'All relatives are a nuisance, though—one must remember that.'

Crispin Maynard came up to our table and said something to Alan. I didn't hear what it was but Alan seemed a little put out. When we were walking home I asked him whether Crispin had said something to upset him.

'Oh, nothing really. He told me he had another article coming out in the next number of Rollo Gaunt's journal.'

'I expect he thought you'd be interested.'

'Oh, Caro, why will you always try to make everything sound so cosy?' said Alan irritably. 'You must know the real reason as well as I.'

I felt crushed and sulky, and we walked on in silence through the complex of modern buildings that looked as if they might have been made from a child's box of bricks with a few neo-Gothic pinnacles jutting up at the corners. Outside there were undulating grassy banks planted ceremonially with very new-looking spindly trees. One of these was a mulberry and it saddened me to think that none of us would live to see it gnarled and venerable or even to pick up its red squashy fruit from the grass.

'That tree isn't doing too well,' said Alan as we passed, and I remembered that Crispin Maynard had planted it.

We crossed a little moat surrounding the library building and I noticed a dead pigeon lying in the shallow water. Another omen? I wondered but did not point it out to Alan.

'Somebody ought to remove that dead bird,' he said after we had passed the spot.

'Yes, or it will putrefy. I expect somebody will— a gardener or whoever looks after the grounds.'

'I always thought it was a mistake having that water,' said Alan. 'It's asking for things to be thrown in it.'

'And someone has scribbled something on the statue,' I added. 'That was asking to be scribbled on, too.'

Alan frowned as we passed a piece of modern sculpture—'statue' was the wrong word—which stood on a little hillock in what had obviously been considered a commanding position. It resembled, and perhaps was intended to be, the lower half of a torso with the thighs spread out. Something had been added to it in red chalk.

'When do people *do* such things?' Alan asked in a worried tone.

'At dead of night, I expect.'

'But there's nobody here at dead of night.'

'Perhaps it wasn't one of the students, then.'

'No, it could have been anybody.' Alan sounded relieved and we reached the car park and got into the car.

Sounds were coming from the undenominational meeting-house which backed onto it. This building was used by the various religious communities in the university. The authorities had hardly liked to provide nothing at all.

'A service *now*?' said Alan, uneasy again.

'It might be some Roman Catholic service—a day of obligation,' I suggested. 'Or perhaps some of Coco's West Indians—the singing sounds not quite English. Anyway, darling, it's nothing to do with *us*.'

When we got home Kate was playing by herself in the hall. She had taken books out of the shelves and had piled them up in tottering heaps which fell as the front door shut.

'She ought to have companions of her own age,' said Alan in a detached way. 'Would you like her to play with Luke and Alice Horniblow?'

'Would *she* like it?' I asked, but this seemed impossible to answer.

V

We are fearfully and won-
derfully made,' Dolly declared, standing up to carve the
wild duck. 'I'll do this without my spectacles because it
is more than I can bear to look at the wonderful cross-
hatched marking on the skin. So you must excuse the
rough-cut pieces.'

'Like Jacobean embroidery, isn't it?' said Menna
Cranton in her lilting Welsh voice. She reminded me of
one of Dolly's hedgehogs, raising up her little face boldly
as I had seen them do when Dolly put out food for
them.

'I believe this marking is called canvas-back,' said
her husband pedantically, 'and one can see that it is apt.'

A brace of mallard had been given to Dolly by Dick Merrilees, a man of about her own age who was an antiquarian bookseller in a neighbouring town and also— or so I always imagined—one of the old lovers who provided such good clothes for her jumble sales in aid of animal charities. He had been invited to eat the duck this evening with Alan and me and Dr. Cranton, the librarian, and his wife. Dolly did occasionally give dinner parties but she very seldom asked Kitty and Coco, for she knew that the sight of her little shop, with its junk-crammed windows and outside book table marked 'All these 5p,' was both embarrassing and painful to them.

'Dear old Doll—sentimental and inconsistent as ever,' said Dick Merrilees. 'Would it be any less upsetting to eat birds with *plain* skin?'

Dolly ignored this and went on carving.

'What trouble the Almighty, or whoever it was, went to,' she said. 'Everything planned in such detail! And yet, Time like an ever-rolling stream . . .'

'Bears all its sons away?' suggested Dr. Cranton, as if he had just hit upon the phrase.

'When one looks back to one's girlhood,' Dolly went on. 'Kitty and I living here as young girls, going to dances and wearing flesh-coloured artificial silk stockings. Kitty used to have hers ironed to make them shiny. *Such* detail and now people wear nylon tights and we shall soon all be gone anyway.'

'Kitty wouldn't like to hear you say that,' I ventured.

'No, she would *not*! If she and Coco had been here I wouldn't have mentioned it.'

I rather doubted if Dolly would have restrained

herself in this way but certainly neither Kitty nor Coco would care to speak of such matters as death and the purpose of life at the dinner table. It cast a gloom over all of us, which was hardly lightened by Alan trying to change the subject by mentioning Crispin Maynard's retirement.

'Yes, his time has come,' said Evan Cranton, not without satisfaction. 'But, of course, my own retirement is two years off.'

'And what do you plan to do then?' asked Dick Merrilees politely.

I could sense a slight hostility between the two men, the opposition of Librarian and Bookseller, no doubt, for I suspected that Evan Cranton had no interest in books for their own sake and did his best to discourage visitors to his library from taking books out of the shelves and reading them.

'Work!' he barked. 'Yes, I shall get down to some real work then.'

There was a puzzled but expectant silence.

'My bibliography,' he said testily. 'My bibliography.'

'Of course,' said Alan, nodding his head in apparent understanding, though I was sure he was as much in the dark as the rest of us as to what exactly this bibliography was.

'Yes, it's nice for a man to have a hobby,' said Menna. 'Especially when he's retired—otherwise he'd be under your feet all day.'

'Oh, Menna is always Hoovering,' said Dolly scornfully.

I was a little shocked at Menna's description of her husband's work, especially when it was a bibliography, for which I had an ignorant superstitious reverence. It looked as if she entered into her husband's work even less than I did.

'Of course, Crispin is having this portrait presented to him,' said Alan.

'Oh? Whose portrait?' asked Dick.

'His own,' Alan explained. 'We in the department are going to present it to him, but I believe a letter is being circulated asking for contributions from others who feel—'

'That they can't get out of sending something,' Evan Cranton interrupted him.

'Well. I think that's nice,' said Menna. 'A nice oil painting to hang in the lounge. Margaret will appreciate that.'

'Who is the artist to be?' asked Dolly.

'Someone from London, I expect,' said Menna.

'My dear, a local artist would hardly be up to it,' her husband said in a crushing tone. 'A portrait is rather more than a pretty water-colour of the hills in autumn.'

'I suppose they wouldn't be able to afford Graham Sutherland or Francis Bacon,' I said, but nobody seemed amused.

We finished the meal and moved into Dolly's sitting room, finding seats as best we could while she made coffee. There was an uneasy silence while she was out of the room, for to settle ourselves at all comfortably various books and objects had to be moved and there was nowhere to put them. To have to do this at all seemed like a criticism of our hostess and I think only Dick Merrilees and I, who knew her best, were unembarrassed.

'Did you see that play about John Aubrey?' Dick asked. 'That stage set reminded me of Dolly's room.'

Evan Cranton held up what looked like a dried hedgehog's skin which he had moved from a corner of a sagging sofa where he had been about to sit.

'What shall I do with this?' he asked.

'Oh, that's nasty,' said Menna in a low voice. 'Some old skeleton.'

'Yes, I found it in a drain,' said Dolly coming into the room and taking it from him. 'Goodness knows how long it had been there—see, it's quite dried, all the flesh gone. What happened to that poor creature? That's what we must ask ourselves.'

'Perhaps it got run over and somebody flung it over your wall,' Alan suggested.

'It may have died of natural causes,' I said hastily, feeling that Dolly was becoming distressed. 'After all, Nature isn't always red in tooth and claw.'

'But the motor car and the man behind the wheel are,' said Evan Cranton and with this talk veered away from the dead creature. Dolly pushed aside some books on the table, put down the coffee tray, then opened a cupboard and took out a bottle of brandy. It was a good brandy and I wondered if it had been a present from Dick Merrilees until she explained that she had bought it with that week's pension money.

Alan looked surprised, even rather shocked. He had a conventional sociologist's view of the elderly and the sort of thing they were likely to, or ought to, spend their pensions on. Brandy was obviously not among them. It was very much in character for Dolly to make a point of telling us that she had spent a large part of a week's pension on a bottle of brandy when she could just as easily have bought it out of her private income or from the money she made from the shop. But she hated to be thought of as a 'senior citizen' and drew her pension aggressively because it was her right, and to annoy and shock Kitty and Coco. Kitty, of course, did not qualify as a pensioner and it was unthinkable to imagine her as one.

'You'd better not tell Sister Dew about this,' Dolly joked. 'She might not approve.'

'No, we'd better not,' said Menna seriously. 'She's quite strict with those old people, you know. An old man fancied a bag of potato crisps—that's what I heard—and she wouldn't let him have them.'

'They might not be good for him,' said Alan judiciously. 'She may have had a reason for withholding them.'

'It was that old missionary—and he's dying anyway, so what harm could a bag of potato crisps do him?'

'You mean Mr. Stillingfleet?'

'I don't know the name. Some missionary who's been in Africa.'

'It sounds as if it must be Mr. Stillingfleet,' I said.

'But potato crisps,' said Alan. 'That seems most unlikely.'

'Nothing's unlikely with old people,' said Menna. 'My old father now. You wouldn't believe—'

'Euthanasia is the answer,' said Evan Cranton and began to outline a scheme whereby the old and senile, or even the old and apparently useless, could be painlessly dispatched, planeloads coming in on package tours from the Continent as they did for abortions.

On the way home Alan suggested that I might take Mr. Stillingfleet a packet of crisps next time I went to read to him.

'I suppose I•could, but it seems a strange thing to take to somebody who's dying.'

'I don't see why. After all, you might take fruit or flowers—what's the difference?'

The next time I went to Normanhurst Alan came with me. Sister Dew let us both go into the room and said that Mr. Stillingfleet was a bit wandering but he had asked if I was coming to read to him and she thought it could do no harm.

I sat down by the bed and introduced Alan as my husband and one who had long admired his work. The old man smiled and nodded, especially when Alan mentioned his book and asked—boldly I thought—whether it was possible to have a look at his original notes.

'What do you want those for?' asked Mr. Stilling-fleet, but then his attention was diverted by the bag of potato crisps and we could not get him to say any more. I began to read, the old man crunched a few of the crisps and then seemed to doze off.

I went on reading, but Alan, who had been sitting on the other side of the bed, got up quietly, went over to the wooden box and opened it. He knew exactly what he was looking for and appeared to find it quickly. I saw him slip a bundle of manuscript into his briefcase, then he shut the chest without making any noise, tiptoed back to the bedside and sat down as if nothing had happened.

After a while Sister Dew came in. She tut-tutted when she saw the potato crisps and I found myself weakly apologising for having brought them.

'Never mind, dear,' she said. 'But I do like to keep my old people looking tidy and crisps are so messy in his beard. It was nice of you to bring your husband.

Now you must both come and have a cup of tea in my sitting room.'

Alan followed me unwillingly, but I felt it was the least he could do, to drink weak tea and eat sweet biscuits in an old people's home, as a return for what he had found.

VI

When we got home Alan shut himself up in his study and I spent the evening watching television with Inge. The next day he told me that thanks to the new material in Mr. Stillingfleet's manuscript his article was finished. I felt pleased that I had been able to help him with his work, though it was hardly the kind of assistance one would see acknowledged in a preface or a footnote.

'What happens next?' I asked.

'I send it to Rollo Gaunt and ask him to consider it for publication.'

Rollo Gaunt, the editor of the leading journal in Alan's field, was a professor at one of our greater universities.

'But he'll take it, surely? There isn't any question of that?'

'Probably not. But one uses the formula.'

'How will you address him—I mean, what do you *call* him? Dear *Rollo*? Or Dear Professor Gaunt?'

Alan frowned and did not answer, appearing absorbed by the niceties of the problem. 'Dear Sir' was out of the question, for Rollo Gaunt was no stranger to him. I knew that Alan had more than once been on the fringe of one of Rollo's post-seminar drinkings, but did he know him well enough to call him by the diminutive 'Rollo'? Apparently nobody ever used his full name—Roland—and the old-fashioned 'My dear Gaunt' form of address was suitable only for an older and perhaps more eminent scholar addressing a younger—certainly not the other way around. 'Dear Professor Gaunt' was possible, but that might give the impression that Alan was thinking too little of himself, was being unnecessarily humble. After all, Rollo Gaunt had only recently got his Chair. It seemed to be a matter of some delicacy.

I went to the window to draw the curtains. It was dark now and lights were showing in the windows of our colleagues' houses, among them Crispin Maynard's study. No doubt the heavy wine-coloured brocade curtains gave that particularly subdued and rosy glow that spoke of snugness and security. It was almost upsetting to picture Alan's enemy—for now that the article was finished, challenging him, I felt that Crispin had become this—safe and cosy, sipping sherry, no doubt, and with no idea at all of what was in store for him. Not that I had read the article, but I felt sure that Alan had 'attacked' him in some way or at least questioned his theories. Quickly, for I felt that I did not want to dwell on that aspect of it, I drew our own less splendid curtains.

I felt even worse the next day when Alan and I took Kate into the town's best restaurant to have tea after the pantomime at the local theatre, for there in the opposite corner at a large round table sat Crispin and Margaret surrounded by grandchildren. There was something at once moving and ostentatious about the sight of the good-looking elderly couple in the midst of such a brood, monopolising the attention of all the waitresses. I, with only one child, felt meagre and inadequate and I suspected that Alan felt the same. Kate seemed particularly prim and self-contained by contrast, commenting smugly and pointing when one of the grandchildren upset his ice cream.

'Naughty,' she said, in the sing-song Swedish accent she had picked up from Inge. 'Naughty little boy.'

At that moment Iris Horniblow came in with Luke and Alice. Alan had not repeated his suggestion that Kate might play with them, and I rather hoped she wouldn't come to our table. Fortunately her attention and that of everyone else in the restaurant was diverted by a loud and apparently unexpected screaming coming from one of her children. Kate again looked smug and cast a sideways glance at me that suddenly reminded me of my mother.

Margaret Maynard came over to speak to us.

'I believe Luke is a difficult little boy,' she said calmly, 'but they usually grow out of it. Of course, children of a broken home do have special problems.'

Meanly I felt rather glad to see the academically brilliant Iris Horniblow at a loss, trying to cope with a fractious child. At last and quite suddenly the child was quiet. Crispin had done something to divert his attention.

'He's wonderful with children,' said Margaret fondly.

'What I really came to say was, *do* watch him on television tonight—he'll be so pleased.'

'Oh, is it tonight?' Alan asked casually. 'We'll certainly watch, won't we, Caro?'

'What's this?' I asked, when Margaret had gone. 'You never told me and you knew all the time.'

'Well, I'd forgotten. He did say something about going up to London to record or film or whatever, some time ago. It's one of those talks on ITV, very late at night.'

When we got home I checked the time of Crispin's talk. It was 11.50, late indeed. Yet we could neither of us resist watching. Familiar though television is, not all that many people one knows appear on it and Crispin was of special interest to us now.

During the evening Alan appeared elaborately unconcerned, but as the time approached I sensed that he was a little edgy and restless, unable to settle to anything. I had the feeling that he would have preferred to watch alone, but I was determined to see Crispin too and had got into my night things so that I should feel comfortable. I wondered if I should suggest a cup of tea or Ovaltine.

'Would you like something, darling?' I asked.

'Oh, tea, if you can be bothered to make it,' said Alan looking at his watch. 'Perhaps we'd better turn it on, it's nearly time.'

He sat stolidly watching an American crime series which I could hear, loud voices and shots, while I made tea in the kitchen. I was out of the room when the opening announcement was made and I came back to find the face of Crispin Maynard looking at me from the screen. Alan watched intently with an occasional mutter of disagreement but I found myself hypnotised by Crispin's appearance and unable to pay much attention to what he was saying. First of all we saw him at a reasonable distance, then the camera moved nearer, bringing the face into alarming close-up so that every detail was magnified.

'Doesn't his hair look *thick*!' I exclaimed. 'Do you suppose he's wearing a toupee?'

Alan made an irritated movement to silence me.

Crispin now began flinging his arms about in what seemed an uncharacteristic manner. I wondered if the producer had told him to do that. It looked rather comic and I wanted to laugh. But after a time I became sleepy and bored.

'Quite well done,' said Alan grudgingly, 'even if one doesn't agree with what he says.'

The credit titles began to roll up and I saw to my surprise that the designer was my sister's boyfriend, Gary Carter. Gary, then, had been responsible for, had 'designed' the setting for Crispin's talk—the heavy 'primitive' table, with the dark-coloured carafe and glasses reminiscent of Casa Pupo and containing—what?

'Rough red wine?' I suggested, as I pointed this out to Alan.

'Water, I should think. Do they call that designing? It hardly seems worth mentioning.'

'Well, it's gratifying to see Gary's name, isn't it. I must remember to tell Sue when I write.'

I shuddered at the idea of Gary, a dark, stocky young man with thick, low-growing hair and a short, bushy beard. I wondered if he was covered with fur all over like an animal. It would be like taking a cat to bed, only much less pleasant.

'What did you think of Crispin's talk?' I asked. 'After all, that's the main thing. That's why we sat up.'

Alan yawned and made a face.

'We must think of something nice to say about it,' I persisted. 'At least he *looked* splendid.'

'I could hardly say *that*, Caro.'

VII

The next day Alan and I heard that Mr. Stillingfleet had died the day after we had been to see him. I think we were both relieved, though we did not say so. His funeral was to be at the crematorium, and Sister Dew rang up to ask if we would like to go. We were both appalled at the idea—Alan particularly. It had not occurred to me that death would of course have to be followed by a ceremony of some kind which one might be expected to attend. I suppose I had imagined Sister Dew disposing of the body in the grounds of Normanhurst, and indeed her tone suggested that she would have been perfectly capable of doing this.

'Cremation, dear, so much cleaner and tidier, don't

you think? I always try to get them cremated if I can. Of course, it's sometimes difficult with Catholics—they don't like it. I was told it's forbidden, bones and relics and that kind of thing. Naturally there would be no difficulty of that sort with the Reverend Stillingfleet. He was *very* low church. And there are no relatives to object, now that the sister's gone.'

'No relatives at all?' I asked.

'No, dear, that's why I wondered if you and your husband . . .'

'I see. Is Professor Maynard going?'

'No, but he's sent a lovely wreath and such a kind message.'

I wanted to know what the message was, but felt I could hardly ask.

'Then there won't be any family mourners?'

'No, just our little party from Normanhurst, and we shall be coming back here for tea afterwards, of course.'

She made it all sound so cosy that I began to wonder if after all it was my duty to go. Alan was making signs at me and I gathered that he wanted me to say that I would. So I agreed to go. Sister Dew seemed pleased, and I supposed it was something of a social occasion for her.

'You'd better order a wreath,' Alan said, 'and think of something suitable to put on it.'

'A kind message,' I murmured. 'I wonder what Crispin put?'

'With deepest sympathy?' Alan suggested, with some lack of originality. Besides, who would the sympathy be for, if the old man had no relatives? I pointed this out.

'Well, it's the kind of thing that's expected. People at funerals don't go too deeply into the meaning of meaning.'

'Some expression of gratitude might be appropriate—for getting that manuscript.'

'For goodness' sake, don't let on about *that*,' said Alan, looking worried. 'Nobody must ever know about that.'

'Well, nobody will if he has no relatives.'

In the end I decided upon bronze and white chrysanthemums and a conventional yet suitable message— 'From Caroline and Alan Grimstone, in remembrance'—for certainly we remembered him. There were only two other wreaths in the hall at Normanhurst, one from the residents at the Home and the other from the Maynards. Theirs was very much the largest and the message on the card was almost fulsome, including homage and gratitude and then some words in a foreign language. Sister Dew told me it was Italian, but it looked to me more like Swahili.

'We didn't know he was so highly thought of by someone like Professor Maynard,' she added. 'It makes a difference somehow.'

We set off in two cars for the crematorium on the outskirts of the town. It was newly built and served a large area of the country around. I remembered going to my father's cremation—the aching throat, tears threatening. Perhaps one could never watch with complete detachment the body sliding away, or hear the words of the address and the strange artificial music without emotion. Sister Dew put her hand on my arm as if to comfort me, and to my dismay I found that I was crying. Nobody else was, and when the short ceremony was over the old people clustered round me as if I was an object of curiosity. I wanted to say that I was not crying for Mr. Stillingfleet in particular but for the general sadness of life and for all of them who would so soon make the journey to this place. I didn't want their kindly fussing and soothing and promises of imminent cups of tea that would make me feel better. When I was eventually confronted by the tea and bridge rolls and a great sticky gâteau I wanted to get away from it all, to be arguing with Alan or playing with Kate or drinking gin with Coco.

'There, there, dear,' said Sister Dew. 'You mustn't upset yourself. If you'd seen as many go as I have . . .'

'It isn't that,' I protested. 'I cry terribly easily— anything sets me off,' I added in as bored a tone as I could muster.

'Oh, I like a good cry at the pictures,' said Sister Dew. 'Or I used to. Some of the disgusting things they show now, and on the TV. You never see what I call a nice film now. . . .'

'And those plays,' said an indignant old woman. 'Filthy, they are.'

But they're not meant for you, I wanted to say, you pathetic old creature with your too-bright lipstick and your raddled old face. Nothing's meant for you now.

'I think watching television's a waste of time,' I said deliberately, knowing it was their one pleasure.

'But did you see Professor Maynard the other night?' said Sister Dew. 'Some of us stayed up for it. Oh, he was *lovely!*'

'Caro, you look terrible, as if you'd been crying or something.'

I had made my escape from Normanhurst and was

on my way home, when Coco came up and took my arm.

'And your clothes! My dear, if I may say so, you should never wear black. It doesn't suit you at all.'

'I know. I've been to a funeral and this old black suit was all I had.'

'Why do people still keep up this silly custom of wearing black at funerals? When I die I shall want people to be looking their best, in their most elegant clothes. Mother looks wonderful in black, of course, but she's an exception. You girls don't know how to make the best of yourselves.'

'I know, darling, you've often told me that. I need a drink.'

'Didn't you get that at the funeral feast?'

'No, only rather a lot of tea and cakes. Oh, Coco, it was awful with those poor old people. Shall we all get like that?'

Coco didn't answer. I knew that it upset him as much as Kitty to think of age and death, and I had been surprised that he could mention his own funeral. But he obviously saw it as an elegant occasion with himself at the centre, not his body grown old and dead and worms eating him.

We sat in a pub in the town and drank gin, just as I had wished in the middle of the funeral.

'I was terribly upset by the whole thing,' I boasted. 'I even cried—it was hideously embarrassing.'

'You and I are sensitive and tender people, Caro. I should have been just the same. What a pity we couldn't have wept together and comforted each other.'

'How *is* your mother?' I asked, thinking of Kitty looking wonderful in black.

'Oh, she's depressed now, even though the relations

have gone. Somehow their coming brought it all back to her—the life *there*, you know.'

'May I call on her on the way back? I'll just stay a minute.'

'Yes, it would cheer her up. She likes to see you, Caro.'

'Even in my terrible old black suit, do you think?'

'Why not? She'll tell you how you could improve it. It might need only a touch of something.'

We had another drink and then came out into the street. The sharpness of the cool evening air was rather too much for me and I realised that I was a little drunk. Coco did not mind that kind of thing and took my arm firmly.

When we got to the flat Kitty called out plaintively.

'Is that you, Coco? Where've you been?'

'I've brought Caro to see you.'

He opened the door and propelled me into the drawing room, which seemed excessively hot after the freshness of the evening. Kitty was lying on a sofa by the window, wrapped in a white quilted housecoat, a fashion magazine lying unopened on her lap. She looked as if she was about to change for dinner. She held out her hand to me and looked me up and down in her usual critical way.

'You don't look well, my dear,' she said, 'and why are you in black?'

I explained about the funeral. This seemed to upset her and I thought it best to change the subject.

'Are you going out this evening?' I asked.

'Only to Dolly's,' Coco answered quickly. 'One has to sometimes.'

'What will you wear?' I asked Kitty.

She looked at me but with unseeing eyes. 'Oh, it

doesn't matter,' she said languidly. 'Do you know, Caro, in the evening now, at about this time, the butler would come and consult me about dinner. "Will you have pink champagne tonight, Madam?" he would ask.'

'Well, Mother, you could have champagne now if you wanted it,' said Coco irritably.

'I know, dear, but it's not the same.'

I could see that it wasn't. Here there was no deferential butler, his black hand concealed in a white cotton glove, pouring champagne for her, ready to gratify her every whim. Coco, of course, would have been ready, too, but, as she pointed out, it was not the same.

'Dolly doesn't notice what one wears,' she said petulantly. 'Or if she does she criticises me for spending too much money on clothes.'

'I must go back to my family,' I said, feeling I was wasting time. And Alan might want to know about the funeral.

Coco came downstairs with me and we stood in the doorway talking.

'Mother's in one of her depressed states,' he said unnecessarily. 'Sometimes she misses it all so much— the servants and the weather—oh, and the garden, of course.'

'Yes, your garden here doesn't amount to much. No bougainvillaea or plumbago or poinciana trees and all those things you told me about. But now it's nearly spring and there are crocuses and snowdrops, even aconites—soon there'll be daffodils, won't there?'

'Will there, Caro? You sound like a seedsman's catalogue. You know how much I dislike Nature as such.'

'I can't imagine your mother actually *working* in the garden.'

'No, but she liked to sit in it and walk round it and

watch the peacocks. Did I tell you how once a peacock got shut up all night in one of the smaller greenhouses?' He shivered. 'The English spring is so cold, anyway.'

'Yes, but it's a lovely time of the year.'

'Caro, you're too young to feel like that about it—spring is only for those who have no hope of anything better.'

'Thank you!' I said indignantly. 'And now I must get home to give Kate her tea.'

Inge had already started to do this and Kate looked up at me critically from her plate of fish fingers and spaghetti hoops. Evidently she didn't like my black suit either. I decided to change it before Alan got home. Now was the time, with spring coming and Kitty's critical appraisal still fresh in my memory, to take stock of myself. I stood before my long mirror in my black slip and dark patterned tights, put on in honour of the late Mr. Stillingfleet. What was wrong with me? Why didn't I ever achieve the look Coco and Kitty seemed to expect?

Before I could do more than formulate this question Alan came into the room holding a letter in his hand.

'I like that dress,' he said. 'Are you going to wear it this evening?'

'It's not a dress.' I opened the letter he gave me. It was from Rollo Gaunt, the editor of the journal to which Alan had sent his article.

I looked at the beginning and exclaimed, ' "Dear Alan"—*that* sounds friendly and cosy!' The letter continued: 'I have read your paper with considerable interest and should very much like to publish it as soon as I can fit it in. You realise, of course, that it may put the cat among the pigeons and I wonder whether it might not be politic to let Crispin M. see it to give him an opportunity of commenting and possibly adding his views at the same time. This would prevent too many bites at the same cherry, since we have, as you of course realise, already published two papers by him on this subject during the past year. If I understand you rightly you have had access to valuable new material which has apparently not been made available to him, and I feel that it is not quite cricket to go ahead without letting Crispin at least have the opportunity of considering a reply. Perhaps you have already done this?'

The second paragraph referred to a few 'minor verbal changes' he had felt obliged to make in certain passages where the sense had seemed to him obscure—he took it that Alan would have no objection to these revisions which would needless to say in no way affect the main argument of the paper.

Alan waited for my reaction. My first one was unsuitable and I suppressed it. Cats, pigeons, too much bitten cherries and cricket seemed to me to give the letter a comic tone but these were irrelevant details.

'It's good that he wants to publish it—he says he's read it "with *considerable* interest",' I said, looking at the letter again. 'Surely he ought not to want to make "verbal changes" though—you write much better than he does, if this letter's anything to go by. But still, he's going to publish it, that's the main thing.'

'Not quite the main thing, Caro.' Alan stood there smiling. 'Does nothing else strike you?'

'Well, you obviously don't want to show it to Crispin Maynard, do you?'

'It's sometimes thought to be a courtesy to do just that.'

'Oh, is it? And are you going to, then?'

'I did try. And what do you think Crispin said?'

'Darling, how could *I* know? That he was too busy or something?' I hazarded.

'That's it—too *busy*. Would you believe it?'

'Perhaps he didn't realise that it was an article on his subject, or perhaps he's lost interest in it—or perhaps he really *is* too busy with his retirement coming soon.'

'He certainly didn't seem to be interested—he said he'd wait until it was published because he didn't see how I could possibly have got access to any new material. Apparently he'd tried to get hold of Stillingfleet's papers last year.'

'Yes, Sister Dew said he's been after them—well, perhaps that's not the way she put it, but I somehow felt he had. What have you *done* with the manuscript, by the way?'

'It's still in my desk. Perhaps you'd take it back to Sister Dew sometime.'

'She might be suspicious, especially as she knows that he didn't want anybody to see the papers in that box.'

'Let's not worry about it now, anyway. What's for dinner?'

'Dinner's too grand a word,' I said. In my mind's eye I saw one of those dehydrated curries or risottos with which young wives in television advertisements surprised and delighted their husbands at short notice. Fresh from the triumph, as it seemed to be, of having his article accepted, would Alan be surprised and delighted, too?

VIII

In spite of Coco the spring came and with it warmer days when Kate could be left in the garden pottering about at her own mysterious ploys, involving mud and sand and water. 'Dirty,' said Inge and Kate echoed her disapproving Scandinavian tones.

One day at breakfast Alan declared that he thought it would be nice if I were to invite Luke and Alice Horniblow to tea.

'Yes, of course,' I agreed unwillingly. Kate sometimes went to play with the Maynard grandchildren and they sometimes came to her but I had taken against Iris Horniblow's children, or, more truthfully, against Iris herself and must have shown a marked lack of enthusiasm as Alan went on.

'They haven't got a garden of their own,' he said reproachfully. 'You know Iris's flat is on the second floor.'

I did know. We had been invited to a wine and cheese party there recently and I was feeling guilty about not yet having returned her hospitality. I remembered the conversation, slightly above my head, the cultured setting with its modern 'objects' and the (to me) unreadable books and Iris's bedroom with the exceptionally wide double bed where I had been invited to leave my coat.

'Do you think Kate would get on with them?' I asked doubtfully.

'That's hardly the point, is it?' said Alan in a patient tone that I knew only too well. 'In any case, Kate mustn't think she's the only person to be considered—the sooner she learns that there are other kids in the world the better, I should think.'

'Oh, yes, obviously,' I agreed. 'But she does play with Emma and Sebastian Maynard, after all—it isn't as if she never saw anybody else.' I was just about to say that of course I would ask the little Horniblows to tea one day when Alan said, 'I think Iris would be very pleased if you did.'

'Oh, if it's to please *Iris*, then I suppose I'll *have* to!' I burst out in a silly schoolgirlish way.

'Caro, *really*, what's the matter with you?'

'Oh, nothing,' I said, on the verge of tears. 'I suppose I'm bored and frustrated and nothing interesting ever happens here.'

Alan rose from the table looking rather pained.

'You know, I wouldn't mind if you got a part-time job,' he said. 'Perhaps that's the answer.'

'Yes, in the library, playing with card indexes from ten to one,' I mocked. 'I can just imagine it. And with Iris Horniblow patronising me.'

In the end, of course, I calmed down and rang Iris. She asked if Luke and Alice could come the next afternoon. This happened to be Inge's day off, but feeling very martyred I said, Of course, that would be fine. Iris brought them in the car and said she would call between half past five and six, if that was all right. She had a seminar that afternoon—she expected Alan must have told me all about the famous Wednesday Seminar. Her face when she left me expressed relief, presumably at having off-loaded her children, mixed with expectation and excitement and the prospect of seeing Alan there.

It was fine enough to put the children in the garden and I did this quite firmly, leaving them to get on together as best they might.

'After all, it's good training for life,' I said to Dolly, who had called in to see me.

'Oh, of course,' she agreed, but not out of interest, for children bored her and in her young days had been segregated from their parents and looked after by nannies. She had come to chat and to cadge jumble for one of her sales. We began talking about Normanhurst and I described Mr. Stillingfleet's funeral, making rather too much of it in the way one sometimes does of a genuinely upsetting experience.

'And all that food afterwards,' I said. 'It was gruesome. How *could* they?'

'Caro, my dear, they were upset, perhaps they were even hungry. You must remember that old people don't have all that much in their lives—certainly not as much as you do.'

'You'll stay to tea, then?'

'What are you having?'

'Hot sausages, little ones, crisps, Twiglets, chocolate cake—but we can have something else if you like.'

When I went out to fetch the three children, they came in obediently and sat without speaking at the table. There was something unnerving about their silence and I was glad that Dolly was with me.

'Did you have a nice game?' I asked feebly. Alice Horniblow smiled in a polite secretive way. Kate turned away and would not meet my eyes. I prepared myself to supervise their slow, messy eating. Dolly had taken her cup of tea and was standing looking out of the window as if she could not bear to watch the children.

'Daffodils,' she remarked. 'Such *obvious* flowers, aren't they? . . . coming before the swallow dares, and all that, and making that other poet's heart fill with pleasure. I can look on them without emotion. But the camellia—that's different.'

'Yes—this is the first year ours has flowered. My mother gave it to us and planted it with her own hands.'

'The clear brilliant colour and dark smooth leaves— and it is scentless, of course. Uncompromising—is that it?'

'I don't know,' I said distractedly, for Luke Horniblow looked as if he were going to cry. Just as he emitted a slow despairing wail, Dolly put down her cup and said she must go.

'The jumble's in the hall,' I said, 'in a paper carrier under the table.'

'Thank you—don't bother to see me out.'

'If you don't mind . . .' I began.

'Of course not—I can see your hands are full.'

For the next ten minutes I tried to get Luke to tell me what was the matter, but without success until Alice explained in a clear bored voice that underlined my stupidity that Kate had hit Luke out in the garden and that was why he was crying.

I wondered what I was going to say to Iris, who was due to collect them at any minute. Luckily by the time she came Luke had stopped crying and was engrossed in a piece of chocolate cake.

'I'm afraid Kate hit Luke,' I confessed. 'It was when they were in the garden. I didn't see exactly what happened.'

'Jolly good for him,' said Iris briskly, but I could see that she wasn't really concentrating. She had flopped down into a chair and sighed in the kind of way that means one wants a drink.

I gave her some whisky, which was apparently what she usually drank. So there we sat, awkwardly at first, drinking Scotch in a most uncharacteristic way.

'I suppose you usually have a drink after the seminar,' I said.

'The men do—the women usually have to rush off to see to children or husbands' meals or what have you. One envies the unattached at such times.'

'They'd be surprised to know that,' I observed, thinking of my sister who was sometimes as bitter as an emancipated woman dared to be about her unmarried state. The TV designer apparently did not count.

'Tell me about Coco Jeffreys,' said Iris. 'I believe you and he are *great* friends.'

'Yes, we are friends,' I began.

'But not lovers, I imagine. No, not that, obviously! What *is* Coco exactly?—I mean, sexually.'

'Well, nothing, really,' I said, embarrassed.

'But he must be *something*.' A note of irritation had now come into Iris's voice—irritation and impatience at my ignorant stupidity.

'You mean hetero or homosexual?'

'Of course that's what I mean,' she mocked. 'Surely *you* must know.'

'We've never talked about it. In any case, are people to be classified as simply as that? Some people just love themselves.'

Iris frowned into her empty glass. I could see my vagueness worried her. Accuracy was as important to her as it was to my sister who, as a social worker, liked to get people cut and dried, neatly classified and pigeonholed.

'Anyway,' Iris went on, 'I'm sure you *are* just good friends, as they say. Why should you want to be anything more when you've got such a dishy husband?'

'You mean Alan?' Really I was being more than usually stupid. It was just that I was surprised to hear Alan described as 'dishy'—embarrassed, too, for it was a word I didn't use myself and couldn't have brought myself to say out loud.

'*I* certainly think so,' said Iris.

'And I'm sure he admires you, too,' I said politely. 'In fact I know he does.'

'Really? What has he said about me?'

The unaccustomed early drink had made me say more than I should. I remembered that Alan had described her as being 'able', which was obviously not what she wanted to hear.

'Don't tell me!' she said, draining her refilled glass. 'Oh, dear, it doesn't need a Gallup poll to find out that drink makes women feel sexy, does it?'

I shrank from the intimacy of agreeing or disagreeing. It was not much use her feeling sexy *here* and at such an early hour, with the children clamouring to be attended to, I thought.

'I hope you'll never find yourself in my position, Caroline.'

I supposed she meant husbandless or unattached.

'It must be . . .' I began, feeling that I ought to say something.

'Not really all *that* bad,' she laughed. 'There *are* people here, after all.'

People here, but who could they be? In my imagination I ranged over everyone I could think of, taking as my field the refectory at lunchtime, seeing them all there drinking and talking shop or going up to the self-service counter for a quick snack. In my mind's eye I stripped them naked and placed them with Iris in her wide bed. But perhaps it wasn't, or they weren't, senior members of the university at all—they might be students or local residents.

Iris was smiling in the polite secretive way that Alice had done.

'Don't look so worried, Caro—may I call you that as everyone seems to—and thanks for the lovely drink. And for entertaining my two horrors.'

I was glad she went quickly before I had time to repeat the invitation for another day. She was barely out of the door before Kate was saying, more as a statement than a question, 'Luke and Alice won't come here again, will they?'

When Alan came in I felt bound to tell him the afternoon had not been an unqualified success.

'Well, you needn't sound so smug about it. I hope you gave Iris a drink when she came to collect them. She must have needed one after the seminar.'

'I gave her two large whiskies. We had a nice talk.'

He looked at me suspiciously and then said, 'I suppose she told you her news?'

'News?'

'She's been chosen to give the Dabbs Memorial Lecture this year—didn't she tell you?'

'No.'

'How modest of her.' So modesty was to be added to her other virtues, I thought.

IX

The pleasure of having his article accepted by Rollo Gaunt lasted Alan for several days. It was by no means his first published work, but the first to be accepted by that particular journal, generally recognised to be the most important one in his discipline, though he had reviewed books for it. The fact that he had 'drawn on unpublished material' that Crispin Maynard had failed to get hold of was now of less significance than what he saw as the establishment of his own position in this particular corner of the academic field. The publication of Alan's article would prove that Crispin had been quite simply wrong or mistaken in his theories; Mr. Stillingfleet's manuscript proved that beyond any doubt. Fortunately I had been kind to the old man and he had allowed me—or my husband, it was the same thing—to make use of his manuscript for scholarly purposes. I was quite sure that that was how Alan now thought of it. I do believe he felt that the responsibility now rested with me. I had the manuscript—he didn't even want to know what I had done with it.

After Easter my sister came to stay for the weekend. The weather was fine and on the Sunday morning we went for a walk in the woods. Alan had declined an invitation to go with us; he didn't like Susan much although he enjoyed arguing with her about the problems she came across as a social worker.

The woods were at the foot of a range of hills for which the town was famous, and people often walked there at weekends, senior members of the university rather consciously taking exercise, many of them even climbing the hills themselves, students tending to lurk in thickets with their girlfriends, and townspeople sitting on the green wooden seats provided by the district council.

Susan and I strode along talking—but she with her longer legs was always a little ahead of me and I would have liked to go more slowly, enjoying the warm gentle sun on my face and listening to the exuberant song of the birds. Perhaps I would have really preferred to walk in silence but her loud clear voice, accustomed to interviewing problem families, held forth about contraception and invited my opinion on other intimate feminine matters. At one turn in the path we came upon Crispin Maynard accompanied by two grandchildren and a large bounding dog which lent an extra dimension of nobility to the picture I already had of him. I remembered Mr. Stillingfleet's manuscript and began to wish that Alan hadn't written his article. I introduced Susan and he said that we looked just like sisters but that Susan was 'a large version of our dear Caro'. I wondered if she would be annoyed at this rather doubtful compliment but she seemed not to notice it and went on with her talk as soon as we had passed him.

We came to a patch of celandines, miraculously untouched, flowers I remembered from childhood.

'Oh, look, celandines,' I said. But Susan didn't even glance at the place I indicated and went on holding forth about some of the more dire aspects of her work from which she was obviously not to be distracted by any false nostalgia for the past. I felt that she was deliberately not letting herself be wooed by the sunshine and the soft air of the spring morning.

We sat down on one of the municipal seats. Susan took out a packet of cigarettes and offered me one of the king-size filter tips she always smoked. Sitting there smoking, I saw that what I had taken to be a violet turned out to be a scrap of purple chocolate wrapper, while an unidentified flower was just a screwed-up pink paper tissue.

'I had an abortion last month,' Susan declared in a clear voice.

'Goodness!' was all I could think of to say. 'Where?'

'In Kilburn—at a private clinic.' Her voice did not drop or falter as she described the event. I could imagine the soft Irish voices of the nurses and hoped they had been kind. But perhaps Susan had no need of kindness.

'Whatever would Mother have said?' I burst out. 'I suppose you didn't tell her?'

'Well, hardly.'

'Couldn't you have had the baby?'

'I considered it, but I couldn't see myself as a gallant unmarried mum. One shouldn't bring a child into the world just because of a moment's carelessness,' she said repressively.

I wondered if she was going to tell me who the father had been. Perhaps it wasn't Gary, the furry TV designer.

At that moment the librarian and his wife came along and I felt guilty in a ridiculous way, hoping they had not heard our conversation.

'Lovely morning, isn't it?' said Menna Cranton.

'Yes, isn't it,' I said, and in spite of everything it was. Evan Cranton raised his hat but made no remark. I was glad that we did not have to make small talk with them.

'I suppose we ought to be getting back,' I said. 'I must put the Yorkshire pudding in, unless Alan's remembered to.'

'Is Alan faithful to you?' Susan asked as we approached the house.

'I think so,' I said, the face of Iris Horniblow coming into my mind.

'Well, if you sound that doubtful he probably isn't.' Susan gave a little laugh. 'What about you, then? Or isn't there anybody here?'

'Not really—and it would be rather awkward even if there were. One would need to be swept away by passion to overcome the difficulties. Besides, the men don't seem to have the time for that kind of thing, so I don't suppose Alan does either. They're always writing reviews or articles or giving lectures and going to seminars and that kind of thing.'

'Don't people sometimes write articles together, men and women?' Susan asked.

'Yes, they do.' This was a new kind of situation I had not thought of before.

Alan appeared at the door as we got back, a book in his hand.

'I told Inge to do it,' he said, showing that his mind had been on the Yorkshire pudding even though he had been writing a book review. I wondered if the finished review would show any of this concern.

Over lunch Alan announced that he had a rather surprising invitation for us for that evening. Crispin and Margaret Maynard were holding a meeting to discuss the possibility or desirability of making a protest to the authorities ('the powers that be' had, apparently, been the phrase Crispin had used) over certain changes that had been made affecting the Third Programme on the radio. At least, this was the gist of it. Alan had some difficulty in making a coherent announcement because he was distracted by Kate upsetting her glass of orange squash.

'But surely it will do if you go, won't it?' I asked. 'Or you and Susan,' I added, thinking it would be a nice diversion for her while I watched a favourite television programme.

'I think we should all go,' said Alan seriously. 'After all, it's important to make one's views known.'

'Views? But you never listen to the radio,' I pointed out.

'*I* certainly do,' said Susan vigorously.

'What time have they asked us to go?'

'After dinner—at least, about nine o'clock. There's going to be coffee.'

'Oh, I see, like one of those parties where one isn't sure if there will be food. I wonder who'll be there.' But, of course, it was not hard to guess. We found the

Maynards themselves and other professors and lecturers and their wives, Iris Horniblow, Evan and Menna Cranton, Dolly, the vicar and, surprisingly, Coco and his mother, both slightly overdressed for the occasion.

'Coffee on a Sunday evening,' Coco whispered to me. 'What does one wear for *that*? People don't seem to have made much effort, do they?'

'They just came as they were,' I said. 'After all, it *is* Sunday evening.'

Crispin clapped his hands for silence. 'Now I expect you've all seen the letter in *The Times*,' he said. 'I think we're all agreed that we should support it, so I'll read out the draft I've prepared. Then we'll discuss it over a cup of coffee.'

'Is that all we're getting?' Coco whispered.

I could see Margaret and Menna Cranton busying themselves with pottery jugs. Margaret's sister Cicely was also assisting. She was the principal of a teachers' training college in the Midlands, a more faded version of Margaret as perhaps befitted an older unmarried sister. I wondered if people would see Susan as a more faded version of me, but of course I knew that they didn't. Susan was forceful in her personality and trendy in her dress. You might have said that she was putting a brave face on things, yet simply being married no longer had its own status—we had long ago given up all that kind of nonsense. But, had we, I wondered, as I watched Kitty twisting the jewelled eternity rings on her wedding finger.

'Mother can't drink out of *this*,' said Coco in a disgusted tone, as the pottery mugs of coffee were passed round.

'They were made by Crispin's daughter,' I said. 'And they always have such very *good* coffee,' I said, sipping mine to encourage him. I noticed that Kitty had put hers down untouched on a side table. She looked helplessly about her and a petulant frown came onto her face when nobody took any notice of her.

Crispin was talking, suggesting a draft for our protest full of suitable phrases: 'grave concern', 'considerable disquiet'. 'Anxiety' was discussed but not accepted— to feel anxiety reflected some sort of inadequacy on our part. Others joined in the discussion with their own suggestions and everything was virtually settled when Dolly stood up and said in her blunt way, 'I hope the old people at Normanhurst are going to be in on this.'

There was a dismayed silence. It was as if Dolly had suggested approaching her hedgehogs for their views.

'I hardly think . . . ,' Crispin began, but I suppose did not like to go on. It was difficult to know what he could say that would be acceptable—obviously the views of a few residents in an old people's home on such a matter were not of the slightest importance or interest, but he could hardly spell it out. 'You see, Dolly, this is really a university matter,' he went on. 'I don't think we shall make our point if we fling the net too wide.'

'I daresay some of the West Indians might have views on it,' Coco suggested provocatively, but no one took any notice of him. The business of Dolly was at once graver and more delicate.

'All this violence upsets them, I know,' Dolly went on. 'I don't think the sex thing—those bare bodies writhing under the bedclothes—really matters to the eighty-year-olds, but it's the violence that's so alarming.'

'But surely you're talking about *television*,' said Crispin gently. 'This petition is concerned with *radio*, more specifically the demise of the Third Programme.'

'Well, I think we should have a good whack at everything while we're about it,' said Dolly.

'What a dreadful old woman,' Susan whispered to me. 'What terrible people you know.'

I found Dolly's outburst upsetting and looked around the room for Alan. I saw that he was refilling Iris Horn-iblow's mug from one of the pottery jugs and that was upsetting in another way. I caught her smiling up at him in the way a smaller woman can to a tall man.

'What was the point of it all?' Kitty asked me plaintively, and I felt that for her the evening had been a disappointment, as indeed so many evenings must be now. And what *had* been the point, really? A few gentle cultured people trying to stand up against the tide of mediocrity that was threatening to swamp them? I who had hardly known anything different could sympathise with their views but for myself I didn't really listen to the radio; I went about my household tasks, such as they were, absorbed in my own broody thoughts.

X

The Dabbs Memorial Lecture was a university function to which I, as Alan's wife, was automatically invited, not so much for the lecture itself as for the drinks and dinner afterwards. It was felt, though never overtly expressed, that Alderman Dabbs, who had left the money to establish this annual event, would not have envisaged ladies sitting in a lecture theatre actually *listening* to a lecture that would certainly be above their heads, but that he would have liked to think of them afterwards in their colourful evening dresses when the conversation would have turned to lighter subjects.

This would be the third Dabbs lecture I had attended. For the first I had bought a new dress. For the second what one wore seemed to matter less and at the dinner afterwards I had sat next to Coco and the lecturer, a young sociologist, at that time unmarried. After dinner the three of us had got rather drunk in the senior common room, the lecturer because his ordeal was over, Coco from force of habit, and I weakly led by their example. This year that young sociologist was married and his wife perceptibly pregnant, Coco and I would not be placed next to each other at dinner, and Iris Horniblow was giving the lecture.

The subject was to be 'patterns of neighbourhood behaviour' in various suburban communities where Iris had done her fieldwork, just after she had graduated and before her marriage. I imagined her in those days in the early sixties, young, handsome, eager—not mature enough to be described as 'able' but with all the potential of a distinguished career before her. And now? As she mounted the platform, introduced by the most senior of the grey sociologists, a spontaneous impulse of generosity made me turn to Alan and whisper, 'Doesn't she look lovely!' He made no reply but did not take his eyes off her and I too found that the pleasure of looking at her made up in some way for the dullness of the lecture. The subject had promised to be interesting—for what could be more fascinating than the study of a community one actually knew?—and at first I tried hard to listen. But after a very few minutes it became apparent that the dead hand of the sociologist had been at work and as soon as I heard the words 'interaction', 'in-depth' and 'grass-roots', I knew that this lecture wasn't going to be any more compelling than the other two had been.

So my thoughts wandered to Iris herself, my first generous impulse evaporated and I found myself studying her with detachment, trying to discover what it was

about her that Alan found so fascinating. Her strong
features, thick hair and large eyes made a powerful
impression and although she was not quite tall enough
her figure was good. She had chosen a very suitable
dress, long and of a dull-surfaced material in a shade of
deep aubergine purple that was almost black. She wore
no ornament but a single rose at the neck of her dress.
As the neck was rather low it seemed that the flower
had been placed between her breasts by a hand other
than her own. Against her rather brown skin it looked
almost like a white rose, but I had the feeling that if I
could have examined it closely I would have found it to
be a very pale pink. We had a rose of precisely that
colour in bloom in our garden and for a moment I had
an overwhelming feeling that it had been Alan's hand
which had plucked the rose and put it where it now
rested. The lecture hall was not dark like the cinema,
but I wished it had been as I instinctively drew myself
away from Alan. Looking at my watch I saw to my
dismay that I would have to sit through at least another
twenty minutes of the lecture before I could hope for
release.

Eventually Iris stopped. She folded her papers neatly
on the reading desk, raised her head and smiled, then
the applause broke out and Crispin Maynard got up to
propose a vote of thanks. Alderman Dabbs would have
been particularly pleased tonight, he felt, and we must
not forget—and he was sure that we would not—that
lecturing and listening to lectures was hungry and thirsty
work, so, with a wide uplifted movement of the arms,
he raised us to our feet and beckoned us to where the
drinks and the dinner were waiting.

'Crispin could have done better than *that*,' Alan
whispered crossly.

'It was very nice what he said, very suitable.'

'Without referring to the subject of the lecture at all? *You* could have done better, Caro. I'm sure you got the gist of it.'

'It was about the behaviour of neighbours. Like the woman who wouldn't feed Dolly's hedgehogs for her,' I said stubbornly, knowing that this was putting it too simply; I was not surprised when Alan didn't answer.

This short conversational exchange had got us out of the lecture hall and into the crush of people surrounding Iris and congratulating her on her lecture. I heard her voice, self-possessed, teasing, almost flirtatious— she hoped it hadn't been too awful and she was (of course) dying for a drink.

Who will get her one? I wondered. Who will be the first to rush to her with the double Scotch? Perhaps it will be Alan.

'*Marvellous* lecture,' I murmured as she brushed past, Alan at her side. Heather Armitage came up to me, followed by Evan Cranton.

'In my day,' he remarked, 'behaviour of neighbours over the garden fence would hardly have been deemed worthy of serious academic study. The trouble is we're running out of primitive peoples so we're driven back on ourselves.'

A waitress passed near us with a tray of drinks and we seized glasses of wine.

'Dr. Horniblow made it all so interesting and worthwhile,' said Heather with her most earnest look. 'It does make one feel that there are opportunities for fieldwork on one's own doorstep.'

'Is Mrs. Cranton here this evening?' I asked, for there was no sign of her.

'No, my wife does not care for this sort of thing,' he said, making me feel that wives ought not to.

After a while we went in to dinner. I had been placed between George Armitage—Heather's husband—and Evan Cranton.

'Ah, we meet again,' said the latter, not sounding very pleased.

'Yes,' I agreed feebly, looking to see if his other neighbour was likely to provide him with more stimulating conversation than mine. It was Margaret Maynard and she appeared to be starting on some topic so that I was free to look around me, George Armitage needing no special attention. I saw that Iris had Alan on one side of her and the young sociologist, last year's lecturer, on the other. There was no sign of Coco, whom I had expected to see at the dinner even if he hadn't bothered to come to the lecture.

'Ah!', said George, as prawn cocktail was placed before us and white wine poured into one of the two glasses that stood at every place, and he began to eat purposefully.

We continued in silence for some time until Evan Cranton turned to me with a question about the old people at Normanhurst. Hadn't I known Mr. Stillingfleet? His wife had mentioned something about him.

'Yes, I suppose Alan and I saw him on his deathbed,' I said, remembering the potato crisps in the beard. 'He was a nice old man. I used to read to him.'

To my surprise Evan Cranton suddenly raised his glass to me in a kind of salute.

'A charming young lady like yourself . . . ,' he began, then stopped short as if with a dawning consciousness of his surroundings and the person he was speaking to. Who, then, had he imagined I was and where were we dining? I could see that a curious intimacy, brought about by the wine and our proximity to each other in the enclosed world we found ourselves in this evening, might develop between us, probably to our mutual embarrassment when we next met. But the likelihood was that he would have forgotten all about it. Only I would remember, as women tend to, smiling or not as the mood took me.

I turned to George Armitage with a remark about the lecture, but he sheered off that subject quickly and began talking about his children without even asking me about Kate. The wine and the surroundings had not made him gallant, intimate or flirtatious. He was, if anything, more than ever like his dull everyday self. He seemed to think it would be of interest to me to discuss his wife's job and how she managed the evening meal. All my charm, or the tiny fragment of it that had been brought out by Dr. Cranton's unexpected behaviour, evaporated, faded away and I became dull and heavy, hardly able to think of a phrase or sentence that would carry George forward to the next dreary stretch of conversation. I found myself thinking of the horrors of marriage into which we entered so glibly. What folly, what courage . . . I looked over to where Alan was sitting next to Iris. He was looking quite attractive. It wasn't saying much, but I think one would have chosen him of all the men present to sit next to had there been any choice.

George had gone on to tell me about the deep freeze he and Heather had recently 'invested in' and the chicken and joints of meat that could conveniently be stored away to be brought out and eaten months later.

'Like mammoth steaks,' I remarked. 'Perfectly preserved in ice after all those years.'

We were rising from the table, and so another Dabbs Memorial Lecture and dinner were over for another year. I wanted to say this to somebody, embroidering the idea, being fanciful, whimsical, even facetious, in the way I could have been with Coco, but there was nobody to listen. As we moved into the common room for coffee and drinks, Alan came up to me, placed his hand on my arm and asked me if I was 'all right'. There could be no answer to such a question. It was a relief when a young American research student came up and asked if he could get me a brandy. I spent the rest of the evening talking to him until people began to leave.

Eventually Alan asked if I was ready to go home. Iris was tired—naturally enough—and we could give her a lift as she hadn't brought her own car this evening. The battery was flat. He could have spared me the last detail, I thought, as I sat broodily in the plastic darkness of our car, but as Iris got into the car I could see that the rose she was wearing was artificial and that made a difference. One couldn't somehow imagine a lover's tender hand tucking an artificial flower into the hollow between her breasts.

'It was a wonderful lecture,' I said in my relief. 'I expect you're glad it's over, though.'

'Golly, yes,' she replied in a schoolgirlish way. 'And Luke and Alice will be too. "Mummy's writing her talk and mustn't be beturbed," Luke used to say. Now Mummy won't have that excuse.' She sighed in an exaggerated way.

'I think your dress is super,' I went on. 'Such a fabulous colour.'

'Thank you,' she said. 'And thanks for the lift, Alan, and all that moral support and Scotch.'

'What a brittle conversation,' I said when we were alone in the car together.

'You and Iris seem to set each other off talking like that,' said Alan, sounding almost puzzled. 'I'm glad you thought the lecture good, though, and praised her dress. That would please her.'

'Yes, praise from another woman is supposed to be particularly pleasing, isn't it? I wonder why?'

'Because they're usually so bitchy?'

I thought of my feeling that wearing an artificial rose belittled Iris in some way and decided that in this instance Alan was right.

XI

My mother-in-law came to stay for a few days and this coincided with the arrival of the proofs of Alan's article, so that one diverted attention from the other. Alan had grown away from his mother, and the excuse of having to correct the proofs kept him in his study in the evenings while Mrs. Grimstone and I watched television. Similarly, my preoccupation with her meant that there was less opportunity for me to share Alan's anxiety over diagrams and groans over printer's errors.

Alan's mother took the whole thing calmly; she knew her son was clever and did not attempt to enter into those superior realms which she saw him as occupying. At times when his cleverness was most obvious she liked to reminisce to me about those days in Liverpool when she was 'carrying' him and how, when he was born, his names—Alan George—had come to her just like that. Alan had always been a favourite name, George was after her husband, killed at Dunkirk, and King George VI. Alan had been the only child and she had not married again. He had been a bright boy, winning scholarships all the way, and when he had met me at university it was only to be expected that he would marry just a little above him.

Katherine Grimstone and I got on quite well together and when we had named Kate, as she thought after her though it was really a name I liked long before I knew her, the bond became closer. There were many things about her that irritated me but in time I had got used to them. She was small, neat and quick, making me feel clumsy, slow and 'dreamy', the last in her opinion the worst of all my bad qualities. Then she would keep on telling me all the things that Alan liked—potatoes and strong tea, bacon cut thick and some particular brand of sauce, most of which I had long since weaned him away from. She spoiled Kate, but only as the kind of little girl she wanted her to be—one who had a great deal in common with children in television commercials—and Kate was cunning enough to go along with her. She would call her 'Nana' to her face and 'Grannie' to me, which made me wonder if she was already showing signs of a brilliant mind that could easily master the subtleties and ramifications of kinship terminology.

One good and cosy thing about my mother-in-law was that she smoked even more than I did. The habit dated from those days in the war and her time of bereavement. I always thought it mean and unfeeling of

Alan when he reproached her for it and we banded together to defy him.

'It's bad for you and a waste of money,' he would
say, stating the obvious. 'Iris has saved up enough to
buy a fur coat since she gave up.'

'Who wants a fur coat?' I retorted. 'It's cruel, anyway, to wear the skins of real animals.'

'Now you're talking like Dolly,' he said, 'and you
know how cranky *she* is. Menna Cranton has a fur coat
and even Margaret Maynard, so it must be all right.'

'I expect Margaret's coat was made from skins ob-
tained in some specially humane way,' I said. 'Anyway
Iris is too short to wear a fur coat—I bet she looks like
a little muskrat.'

'How is the book going, Alan?' asked his mother.
'Have you finished correcting it?'

'It isn't a book, Mother,' said Alan patiently, 'just
an article that will appear in a journal.'

'Oh, I see, like in a magazine.' Mrs. Grimstone
nodded and adjusted the thing at the end of her knitting
needle that showed she had done another row.

'Yes, I suppose one could call it a magazine, couldn't
one, Caro?'

He was smiling his superior smile so I said, 'Yes,
one could. Only it's rather less readable than most.'
Then repenting, I added, 'I hope the article has come
out reasonably well—not too many mistakes?'

'They've messed up one diagram rather,' he said,
'which is a bit worrying. I'm not sure what to do with
it. Oh, and darling,' he took me to one side and said
quietly, 'seeing that the article's finished I suppose Stillingfleet's manuscript ought to be returned. You might
slip it back for me and fix things with your friend Sister
Dew.'

'*My* friend—she isn't that exactly, but I'll take it along.'

It would be an excursion for Mrs. Grimstone, or Kath as she liked to be called, to visit the old people's home, and Sister Dew would probably offer us some refreshment.

'. . . that's the *strong* one, they say. Kills all known germs *dead*. And it's what we use here. You can't be too careful with old people.' Sister Dew smiled and replaced the knitted cosy on the teapot. It was silly and squeamish of me, I knew, but her conversation about the hygienic precautions taken in the 'toilets' at Normanhurst did rather put me off my tea.

Mrs. Grimstone nodded and I could see she was making a mental note to get some of this particular disinfectant for our lavatory, for she too had heard it praised on television. It was her custom to present me with such unusual 'gifts'.

'*And* where there are kiddies,' she added.

'Is anyone else in Mr. Stillingfleet's room?' I asked.

'Oh, bless you, *yes*. The day after he died there was someone in that bed.'

'Who?'

'A lady—she'd been on the waiting list for some time. Her son and daughter-in-law brought her along as soon as they heard Mr. Stillingfleet had gone, almost *too* soon, before we'd had time to get the room ready. Would you like to see her? I expect she'd be glad of a visitor.'

I hesitated and must have seemed to shrink back, but Mrs. Grimstone answered quickly for me that of course we'd like to see the lady. As we got up to go into the room I realised that I had put my shopping bag with the manuscript in it under my chair. I took it with me, hoping that I might somehow replace it in the box of the old missionary's effects, but when we entered the room I saw that it looked quite different. The furniture had been moved around and there was no sign of the wooden box with its heavy strap where Mr. Stillingfleet had kept his things.

A rather stout old woman was lying on rather than in the bed, as if having an afternoon nap. She was covered with a red-and-blue-checked rug, making her look like a red and blue mountain. Spread out around her were bundles of cigarette coupons done up with rubber bands.

'Counting your treasure,' said Sister Dew in a rather loud, jolly tone. 'She's deaf,' she added. 'She likes playing with her cigarette coupons and deciding what to get, don't you, dear? Now we must get ourselves tidy and go down for tea, mustn't we? Put the coupons away—there now. I've brought some visitors to see you.'

The woman looked up at us blankly.

'What happened to Mr. Stillingfleet's things?' I asked. 'The papers, I mean.'

'Oh, that Dr. Cranton from the university library took them,' said Sister Dew. 'I was glad to be rid of them, I can tell you. I didn't like to burn them.'

'Had he any right to take them?' I asked.

'Oh, they were going into the university library,' said Sister Dew in a reverent tone, 'so that must have been all right. The old man would have been pleased about that.'

'Yes, I suppose he would,' I said slowly, wondering how I was going to return the manuscript now. Alan had laughed when I said that I was afraid of Evan Cranton, but it was true. I couldn't see myself going to him

and handing over the manuscript and, as I had no idea
where all the various manuscripts were kept, there was
no chance of sneaking it in somehow. It never occurred
to me that Alan might return the manuscript himself.
It had seemed, from the beginning, somehow my responsibility.

When we got home Alan told me he had decided
to go up to London the next day—something to do with
his article. He felt he had to see the assistant editor about
the diagram that was wrong. It seemed such a peculiar
reason that I began to wonder whether he had secretly
arranged to see Iris Horniblow in town. It was ridiculous
to have such a suspicion, but it would not leave me and
in the end, after he had gone, I rang her flat. There was
no answer; she was obviously out. Of course, she might
have been teaching or taking her children somewhere.
On an impulse I rang Coco. He was his usual cosy self
but not at all reassuring about Alan, which was the main
reason I'd rung him.

'Caro, men *do*,' he said earnestly, as if I didn't know,
'and that Horniblow woman is just asking for it. I wonder where they would go,' he speculated. 'One of those
hotels where you can take a room for the afternoon?
Unless they know someone whose flat they can borrow.'

Alan arrived back by the last train, which got in at
eleven. Mrs. Grimstone and I waited up for him, or
seemed to be doing so, as we sat silently in front of the
television. She was, as always, knitting some garment
for Kate. Of course, it wasn't really late but there was
a feeling of tension in the air. Alan's dinner had been
waiting in the oven, since I had no idea when he would
be back, and even the slowest-cooking casserole, which
it had been, might be expected to have dried up by now.
I think we both felt a kind of satisfaction about this, but

we were quickly deflated when Alan announced that he had had dinner on the train.

His mother pursed her lips and I could almost hear her saying, 'Waste of money.'

He looked rather pleased with himself and at his most attractive.

'Was the business about the diagram settled all right?' I asked, bringing the words out with difficulty.

'Oh yes—rather a stupid assistant editor, but we got it right in the end. That's always satisfactory.' He smiled in a way Kate sometimes did.

'Did you see Rollo Gaunt?'

'Yes, we had a drink together.'

'Not dinner?'

'No, I told you—I had dinner on the train.'

I tried to remember what the classic signs of infidelity were: a long hair on the collar, a lipstick mark on a handkerchief or the hint of an unfamiliar scent—they all seemed rather old-fashioned.

All I could think of to tell Alan was that Dr. Stillingfleet's papers had found their way into the hands of Evan Cranton, but he seemed uninterested and I began to wonder if we were to be saddled with the manuscript forever like a kind of albatross.

XII

A few days later we were sitting at breakfast when Alan looked up from *The Times* and pointed out an item in the Deaths column. The name Esther Clovis meant nothing to me, but Alan seemed to think that I ought to know about her. He told me that she had done very important work at some research centre in London which used to send people out to do fieldwork in Africa and other suitable places in the days when there were still 'primitive communities' to be investigated by anthropologists.

'It says here "suddenly",' I pointed out. 'And there's to be a memorial service next Wednesday—are you going to it?'

'Caro, how could I, on a Wednesday of all days?'

'Oh, of course, the Wednesday Seminar. But you wouldn't go anyway, would you?'

'I don't know, but I feel one ought to pay some kind of tribute. Various people will be there . . . It would be expected . . .' He hesitated. 'I know—*you* can represent me. You'd enjoy a jaunt to London, wouldn't you?'

'Well, not to a memorial service. Still, I suppose it won't take long.'

'You could arrange to meet a friend for lunch afterwards,' Alan suggested. 'One of those girls you were at school with.'

'That sounds absolutely super,' I mocked. 'Thanks, but I don't think I'll bother. I might pick up an interesting anthropologist.'

'Certainly, darling,' said Alan in a hurtful, not caring, sort of tone. 'You could buy yourself something new for the occasion.'

'Yes, I'm certainly not going to wear that old black suit I wore at Mr. Stillingfleet's cremation. There, you see, this will be the *second* occasion when I've represented you at this kind of thing. It wasn't quite the role I saw myself filling when I married you,' I added with some bitterness.

But Alan wasn't listening and went off murmuring something about Esther Clovis not caring a bit what anyone wore so I might just as well please myself.

It was a beautiful church, the one chosen for the memorial service. Services of this kind were quite often held there because of its convenient situation. The architecture was eighteenth century and there were some fine monuments and wall tablets, handsome pews and shining brasswork, and a clean smell of cold stone and lav-

ender furniture polish. I was a little disappointed that
there was no whiff of incense, no popish darkness or
hint of Continental squalor.

On a low table facing the congregation was a striking arrangement of carnations and delphiniums, of the
type often seen in the foyer of an expensive block of
flats or an advertising agency. There was no sign of any
coffin or urn containing ashes so it wouldn't be at all
upsetting, and I prepared to enjoy myself with detachment. Not having known Miss Clovis, I could not be
expected to feel sorrow.

The church was quite full and there seemed to be
more men than women, which must have been unusual
compared with an ordinary service. My clothes—a dark
blue suit with the new longer skirt—seemed just right,
even a little too smart, and that gave me a feeling of
well-being unusual these days. There were some rather
non-committal hymns on a printed service sheet which
was headed 'Esther Ivy Clovis 1899–1970' in Gothic
lettering. A clergyman, perhaps the vicar, said prayers
and then we sat down for the address which was given
by a layman, Professor Digby Fox, presumably an anthropologist, though his name was not familiar to me.

You might think that this elegantly formal setting
was not what she would have chosen, I was told. These
lovely flowers would have made her smile—she whose
only concession to floral decoration was a roughly gathered bunch of bluebells thrust into an old jam jar. We
were invited to picture Esther in her home, a setting so
very different from this one in which we were gathered
to remember her. Yet there might come into our minds
the words of the hymn 'For it is seemly so to do' and
that was the point of our being here. Esther expected
the best from others and deserved it now from us. She

abhorred slipshod work of any kind; indeed, some of us felt that she was still with us, looking over our shoulder, reaching out to us from beyond. Her advice to young people about to enter on a period of field research might often have seemed harsh, as was her criticism of written work that failed to reach the high standard she expected. One thing we know would have pleased her and that was the manner of her going—suddenly, you could almost say brusquely, reminding us of her own manner of bringing something to an end which, in her opinion, had gone on long enough. The speaker felt sure that Esther Clovis would have dealt in this way with his own faltering words and he proposed therefore to say no more, only to add that a scholarship was to be endowed in her name and that donations would be received at the back of the church after the service.

We stood up and sang 'He who would valiant be', all of us, I think, a little shaken. My impression was that Miss Clovis had not been a very nice person. She had obviously not been a Christian, so why had they had a church service? The words 'For it is seemly so to do' came back to me and I suppose one might have thought that it was not only seemly but politic.

I did not imagine that I would have to do anything about making a contribution to the scholarship fund, though I would tell Alan in case he felt he ought to contribute, but when I reached the back of the church I found that it was impossible to get out before I had given my name to the woman sitting at a table.

'Caroline Grimstone,' I murmured. 'I'm representing my husband, Dr. Alan Grimstone.'

'Was your husband not able to come?' she asked rather sharply.

'No, he had a seminar,' I explained, feeling that it

was an inadequate excuse, but to my relief the woman nodded her head in approval and I realised that of course Miss Clovis would have understood.

Outside, the mourners, if such they could be called, and those who had come to pay their respects stood in little groups. One cluster of men in early middle age made straight for a nearby pub and I wondered if they had been particularly affected by the thought that Miss Clovis was even now reaching out to them and needed a drink that much more.

I had made no plans for myself, done nothing to get in touch with an old school friend as Alan had suggested. It was a quarter to one and I felt I deserved a good lunch, though it had started to rain so I didn't want to go far. I supposed I must be somewhere near Soho and was just about to cross the road and go in a likely direction when somebody took my arm and called my name.

'*Caro!* It *is* you, but of course.'

'Why, David . . .'

It was my first love, still Byronic-looking and now, I had heard, something to do with the Conservative Central Office. His face looked no older than at our last meeting eight or nine years ago and the dark curling hair, which had then been thought eccentrically long, now appeared quite ordinary.

A rush of memories came back to me.

'Caro, my *dear*—we must have lunch together, if you're free.'

I was free, but how could *he* be? Surely some arrangement had fallen through, some person not materialised, I thought, as I sat with him in the Soho restaurant, drinking in a dark intimate little bar while he pored over the menu.

After the first surprise, astonishment and pleasure of being together again, what was there to say? He told me he was not married yet and I had the feeling that he was waiting to find somebody 'suitable'. I told him about Alan and Kate and tried to make life in a provincial university town sound amusing. David was not exactly listening but he paid me compliments and said my name rather too often, his eyes widening as he looked at me.

'You were always very sweet,' he said in an elegiac tone.

'So were you.' The seductive atmosphere of the restaurant, the effect of the wine and the face opposite made me wonder why on earth I had married Alan when there were still men like this about. Perhaps I should have waited until I found another David.

'Darling, it wouldn't have worked,' he said, his voice heavy with regret, yet also almost cosy with the knowledge that it was too late to do anything about it now.

'Of course not,' I said.

I wished I were in a novel or even some other person's life where we could have gone back to his flat or to a hotel, sleazily romantic with heavy dingy lace curtains—the kind of place Coco thought Alan might be taking Iris Horniblow. But when we had drunk our coffee David looked at his watch.

'Time to go darling,' he said. 'Alas.'

'Yes—one must go.' I turned my head away as he took out what seemed rather a lot of money to settle the bill. I was glad it had been an expensive lunch.

'What will you do now?' His handsome face looked almost concerned, as if he minded. 'Perhaps I could drop you off somewhere?'

'Paddington,' I said flatly.

He smiled. 'Well, I'm not exactly going in that direction—somehow one never is.'

'Why not?' I asked crossly. 'What's wrong with Paddington? One goes to some very desirable places from it.'

'Oh, you mean Paddington *Station*—yes, I see.'

On this ludicrous little misunderstanding we parted and I sadly went down the steps of the nearest Underground and bought a ticket for Paddington.

In the tube train I practised my sister's technique of observation, looking at the people in the carriage and taking in the details of their appearance as if I were a sociologist or even a novelist storing useful material. A woman in a Burberry, reading *The Economist*, good leather handbag; another, middle-aged, pretty, hair going grey, that untouched virginal look, has never, perhaps . . . probably too late now; a man, youngish, correctly but uninterestingly dressed, with new square, status-symbol-type briefcase; others, even less worthy of notice, with sad, tired faces. When did the joy begin to go out of their lives, I wondered, and why were they travelling in the middle of the afternoon? Life's journey, Dolly might have said.

At Paddington I had a cup of tea and found a corner seat. I was sitting looking out of the window when I saw Heather Armitage hurrying along the platform, looking for a seat in the already full carriages.

'A day's shopping,' Heather declared unnecessarily, as she was weighed down with several large carrier bags. 'And what have you been up to?'

'Attending a memorial service and lunching with an old lover.'

'*Caroline!*' Obviously Heather didn't believe me—at least not the lunch part.

'There was a service for someone called Esther Clovis,' I said. 'Alan thought one of us ought to go.'

Heather's face clouded over. 'Oh, dear, I wonder if *I* ought to have gone. George never mentioned it. What *was* she—I mean, what did she *do*?'

'I don't know exactly—something to do with a research centre.'

'Was she a librarian?' Heather asked anxiously.

'It wasn't mentioned at the service.'

Heather was obviously relieved, but then she feared that Miss Clovis might have compiled an important bibliography which would require that homage be paid to her after death.

'George would know, of course,' she said, 'and these things might be considered a wife's duty, don't you think? I mean, attending a memorial service is the kind of thing one can easily do for one's husband.'

'How inadequate we must be, if that's all we can do,' I said, but when I got home I wondered if Heather was not right after all, for there were Iris Horniblow and Alan in our sitting room having a drink 'after the rough and tumble of the Wednesday Seminar', as they put it.

'I expect Caro needs one, too,' said Iris kindly, 'if she's been to the Clovis memorial service.'

She seemed to be talking rather a lot, more than was necessary. I talked a lot, too, describing the service in detail and making much of my lunch with David afterwards. I reflected that if more had happened I would have kept it secret and that Iris must realise this.

'Poor girl,' said Alan, after she had gone.

'You're having an affair with her!' I blurted out. I had meant to challenge him some time, to do it subtly, but such situations are difficult to act out and this particular one was so hackneyed that it is almost impossible to interpret it freshly.

'With Iris?' Alan seemed genuinely surprised. 'She's certainly very able, but I wouldn't want to go to *bed* with her.'

This was comforting, but somehow I still didn't believe him. There was a silence. Alan stood up and began pacing about the room as people do in literature.

'Caro, there *is* someone,' he said, 'but it's not Iris.'

For a moment I felt so relieved that I could only take in the last part of what he had said. *Not* Iris Horniblow—I glowed with triumph. Then, of course, I realised the full implication of it not being Iris. There *was* somebody and it was somebody else. But who could it be? One of his students or someone equally humiliating for me?

'Caro,' he went on, 'you remember when I went up to London to sort out the balls-up they'd made of that diagram in my article?'

'Yes, of course I do. Did you meet someone there— on the train or somewhere?'

'Not on the train.' He smiled. 'Rollo Gaunt's assistant editor, or whatever one calls her—that stupid girl who messed up the diagram.'

He sounded foolishly doting and I was sickened as much by that as anything else.

'But when and *where*—not in Rollo's office, surely?'

'No, not there. She has a flat.'

'How convenient. How old is she and what's her name?'

'She's called Cressida—about your age. She's a hopeless sort of person, though'—as if I were not also that.

'With a name like *that*—' I began in a bitter tone.

Then Inge came into the room after her evening out. She had been to the au pairs' club and was wearing her national costume. Alan paid her a joking compliment.

When we went to bed I expected Alan might sleep on the divan in his study, which we used as a spare room, but he seemed not to feel that any change in the usual pattern was called for. I lay stiffly on my side of the bed, so near to the edge that I was in danger of falling out. We neither of us spoke until Alan put his arms round me and told me that this kind of thing couldn't possibly make any difference to us—it might even be a kind of enrichment of our marriage. But there seemed nothing that I could say in reply that would not sound false.

XIII

The next morning I awoke with the feeling that something was different. Then I remembered what had happened and was astonished to realise that I had slept at all. Alan had been unfaithful to me and I thought that if it had happened sooner I could have discussed it with Susan.

I got out of bed very carefully without disturbing Alan and went to the window. The church clock began to strike. I counted and found that it was only six o'clock. Had it been seven I might, indeed could, have found something to occupy me, but six o'clock was not an hour in our lives, though it often was in Kate's. I paused at the door of her room as I crept downstairs, hurriedly dressed in jeans and a shirt, but there was no sound.

When I got outside there was nobody about and I felt as one might if the world had come to an end. There was a freshness in the air and a feeling of expectancy, but the stillness and solitude were broken by a bent cassocked figure hurrying into the church on the corner. Surely there couldn't be a service at *this* hour, I wondered uneasily.

My first waking thought had been to get away from Alan; I now wondered what I should do next. Coco would be a sympathetic, even eager, listener, I knew, but to pay him a surprise visit at such an early hour was out of the question. Neither he nor Kitty would be equal to it. I remembered him once telling me, as if I couldn't have guessed, that they were neither of them at their best in the morning. He had quoted something out of an old *Vogue* to the effect that like most of us past the early rosebud age he was no great beauty at dawn or thereabouts and I suppose the same must apply even more to Kitty. Dolly was the obvious person to go to and I knew she would be up and busy on such a fine day. I turned in the direction of her cottage, beginning to feel the need for coffee as well as sympathy. Yet when it came to the point, what could I tell her?

'Good morning, Caro, this is a delightful surprise!'

Crispin Maynard stood before me with dog and grandchild, a Wordsworthian figure. My first feeling on seeing him was of dismay, for I had not expected to meet anyone that I knew, but then I realised that older people like Crispin and Dolly always woke early and all I had to say was what a lovely morning it was and agree that this was the best part of the day.

We walked along together and I wondered where

he was going. He might equally have wondered about me and when he explained that he always gave Prince a run in the woods in the early morning I felt at a loss for a similar explanation of my own early rising. After all, my circumstances were a little unusual, or at least I hoped they were. Having run away from Alan on this first morning I had made no plans as to what I should do on future mornings.

'What do you do when it rains?' I asked.

'Put on my Burberry,' said Crispin cheerfully. 'It makes no difference to Prince.'

Nor would the weather make any difference to whatever I was taking out for a walk this morning. Wet or fine it would still be with me.

'What will you do about brekker?' Crispin asked, looking at me with kindly concern.

'Brekker?' At first I couldn't think what he meant, then when I realised I said I would have something with Dolly.

He looked doubtful. 'Can you last out that long?' he asked. 'Margaret will have something ready now, you are very welcome.'

I was sure I would be, but the idea of facing somebody so well balanced and splendidly organised when I was in such a low state and looking so terrible was too much for me.

'Dolly will be expecting me,' I lied. 'Something to do with the hedgehogs. You can sometimes see the baby ones early in the morning.'

'Kate would enjoy that,' said Crispin, 'and so would Emma.' He indicated his gambolling grandchild. 'We must organise something another morning.'

'Yes, we must,' I said. 'Do give my love to Margaret.'

'And you tell Alan that I am looking forward very much to reading his article. You know he offered to let me see it in manuscript,' Crispin added in a confidential tone. 'But, my dear Caro, it bores me so much now, reading things in manuscript or galley proofs, awkward slippery things. I'm getting to the age when I prefer to read things decently in print. You tell Alan that.'

I thought guiltily of Mr. Stillingfleet's manuscript upstairs in a drawer in my dressing table, hidden beneath my scarves and belts like a naughty book in the dormitory at school.

By the time I got to Dolly's cottage I was worn out, physically and emotionally, and when she asked me why I had come at a quarter to seven in the morning I burst into tears and gave her an incoherent and slightly exaggerated account of what had happened. Afterwards I was a little ashamed and felt I had been disloyal to Alan in betraying his secret and also selfish in not realising that Dolly was upset about something too. It appeared that one of the hedgehogs—her favourite— had not come for its food for some time and that only this morning she had found its dead body in the leaves.

We sat drinking cups of instant coffee and smoking, commiserating with each other. An unfaithful husband and a dead hedgehog—sorrows not to be compared, you might say, on a different plane altogether. Yet there was hope that Alan would turn to me again while the hedgehog could never come back.

'There'll be another,' I said.

'Yes, but not my golden Maeve, the ancient Irish queen,' Dolly lamented. 'Would you like something to eat?'

'No, I suppose I'll be home for breakfast. But what am I to *do*? Oh, Dolly, I never thought he really would.'

Dolly looked at me with her remotest expression, then narrowed her eyes in a characteristic way as if she were trying to remember what it had been like in the thirties when her lovers were unfaithful. But perhaps they never had been. After all, one of them still gave her his old clothes for her jumble sales.

'It shouldn't affect your marriage,' she said at last. 'After all, the main relationship is still there. It may even add something to it.'

She was saying very much what Alan had said in bed in the small hours. I felt ignorant and unworldly and that I should know better another time. Perhaps Kitty would have understood better, the personal humiliation of having someone else preferred to you.

I left Dolly brooding over the dead hedgehog and quoting Yeats. For the first time since I had known her I felt she had failed me. Obviously it was too much to hope that people still went on feeling things with the same intensity over the years.

When I got home they were at breakfast, or rather at the breakfast table. The milk for the coffee which Alan was supposed to be watching had boiled over and he and Inge were busy with cloths. There was a horrible burnt smell.

'Milk has overboiled,' cried Inge and Kate, sensing excitement in the air, beat with her spoon on her cereal dish.

'You should have used the glass marble thing Mother gave us,' I said coldly.

'What thing and whose mother—yours or mine?'

'Yours, the last time she was here. You put it in the pan and it stops things boiling over.'

'Oh, well . . .' Alan made a helpless gesture with his cloth. 'Where have you *been*?' he asked in a low voice.

'I went for a walk and called to see Dolly,' I explained, surprised and pleased at the calmness that had come over me.

'Yes, I guessed you might have been. She's the only person I could think of who'd be up so early.'

'So you did think.'

'Certainly—I thought and I wondered.'

Inge came in with the coffee. She looked fine and solid with her shining blond hair and aquamarine eyes. I wondered if Alan had ever approached her or crept up to her attic to make love to her. I saw him dispassionately as a monster of lust—Inge, Iris, this girl in London—how many others might there have been?

'How was Dolly?' he asked, as if he cared.

'Her favourite hedgehog died,' I said.

Kate's face crumpled and she let out a loud wail. I had been careful to teach her about death through the medium of birds and small animals and we had interred quite a number in shoe boxes with moss and flowers.

'Died,' she howled.

'Is dead the little hedge-pig,' said Inge.

Alan threw a sideways look at me but I just went on eating toast. At last Kate was quiet and Inge took her away.

'I met Crispin on my walk,' I said. 'He's looking forward to reading your paper when it comes out. It's a pity he won't still be in Italy then—he'd just leaf through the journal idly sitting on his *terrazza* drinking vermouth and it wouldn't mean a thing that you've got all this new material that he couldn't get hold of himself.' I found myself in tears.

'Caro, it doesn't matter. Can't you understand that it doesn't really affect us?'

'I must go away,' I said. 'I'll take Kate to stay with

my mother and Inge can go back to Sweden earlier.'

'Well, if you like,' Alan agreed, 'but you know your mother irritates you, and will you really want to cope with Kate without Inge to help you?'

'Then I'll get a job,' I said defiantly. 'I'll go to the library and ask Dr. Cranton to take me on in the mornings.'

'I'm sure he'd be glad to do that,' said Alan, 'but don't do anything in a rush, Caro. Don't get involved in something you don't like.'

'I don't know what I like or don't like till I've tried it,' I said childishly.

I went upstairs to our room. It seemed an outrage that I should be expected to make our bed so I left it unmade. It looked defiant in its wanton untidiness. I put on some more respectable clothes and did something to my face. Then I rang up Coco and invited myself to lunch. He seemed almost excited at the thought of seeing me. Could he have heard something already? I wondered.

XIV

D olly called Mother,' Coco
explained. 'She said you'd arrived at her cottage at seven
o'clock in the morning in a distressed condition. *A distressed condition*,' he repeated with emphasis, 'those were
the very words she used. So naturally we wondered and
I hoped—expected—you'd call me. I was waiting by
the telephone.'

We were having lunch in the country some miles
outside the town, not in one of the old unsophisticated
pubs where one could still eat bread and cheese with the
locals, but in a tarted-up place where American tourists
called on their way to Hereford and Wales, to enjoy
well-cooked English food in carefully arranged antique
surroundings with discreet gusts of warm air coming

from behind panelled walls, even though it was a summer day.

We had driven here almost in silence and had a drink at the bar, still without anything other than trivialities being spoken. Now, away from other people, at a corner table, I could feel Coco's eagerness to be confided in, to learn what had made me call on Dolly at seven o'clock, to know *all*.

'In a distressed condition . . .' The words seemed to fascinate him. 'Caro, it isn't *like* you. I wondered if anything could have happened to Kate?'

'Yes, something happening to one's child would be the first thought,' I agreed, realising the fact of my motherhood.

'But then I said to Mother, if it had been Kate you wouldn't have called and asked me to take you out to lunch—you'd have wanted to be with her.'

'Yes, that would be the natural behaviour of a mother, I suppose,' I said doubtfully. 'No, Coco, it was Alan. We've had a row.'

'Oh.' He sounded disappointed. 'I thought it was something much more serious than that.'

'Alan and I don't have rows—it *is* serious for us.'

'But what *about*? Caro, you must tell me. How can I help you if you don't tell me *everything*?'

A waitress came to take our plates away. I had hardly eaten anything and felt ashamed of the meat I had toyed with and left on my plate. Perhaps some animal in the kitchen would appreciate it.

'Let's have ice cream,' said Coco childishly. 'And what do you want to do afterwards?'

'Go for a walk, I think. One can't really talk here.'

Coco would have preferred to sit in the car, but he followed me reluctantly along a path at the back of the pub and into a wood. With his dislike and fear of Nature I hardly expected him to enthuse over the beauty of the drifts of bluebells and delicate green of the uncurling fronds of the young bracken.

'Now you can tell me,' he said when we came to a little clearing which seemed suitably remote. 'Nobody will hear us in this glade.'

'I don't know if I *can* tell you,' I said, flinging myself down.

'Caro, isn't the ground damp? It must be. What are we going to sit on?'

I was wearing a light summer coat which I took off and spread on the ground.

'Won't it spoil your coat, putting it on the damp grass?'

'It doesn't matter—and it isn't all that damp.'

Coco sat stiffly, as if preserving himself, and I lay back and looked up into the branches of a tree, seeing the sky through a tracery of leaves. It pleased me and I would have enjoyed the silence and peace with Coco, without having to talk, but I could feel him eager still, ready to help me on with his questions.

'Has Alan been unkind to you? Is it anything to do with Iris?'

'In a way.'

'He hasn't struck you—used violence?'

'Alan?' I smiled at the idea and my smile seemed to irritate Coco.

'According to Dolly it was something dreadful— something that had upset you very much.'

'He told me that he'd been to bed with a girl in London,' I said crudely.

'*Caro!* A prostitute? But *why*? Nowadays it isn't

necessary to do that with girls so much more obliging. Oh, I see—it *was* Iris and they went to a hotel in the afternoon, as I thought they might! You remember I told you that men did things like that.'

I closed my eyes. I wished Coco wouldn't talk so much and with such detachment. I heard him going on about the practical difficulties of such a situation and speculating whether it was possible to take a room for such a purpose at the Savoy or the Hilton or that hotel in Kensington by the Antique Hypermarket (Caro, dear, just imagine *that*!). Or did such places have to be in seedy, run-down areas near main-line railway stations?

'It wasn't Iris,' I said, thinking I had better make that clear. 'It was a girl he met, not a prostitute, and they went to her flat.'

I wished now that I hadn't said anything at all about it, but it was too late and I was punished for my indiscretion and disloyalty by not finding the consolation I had hoped for. What I needed was to be fussed over with loving words and tender gestures, but I could hardly have expected that from Coco. Yet now he was bending over me; there was concern in his dark eyes and his face had come close to mine. I waited in surprise and embarrassment, for I realised that in this kind of situation Coco meant nothing to me. I held my breath wishing he had not come so close.

'Caro,' he said anxiously, 'there's an insect on your gown. Let me brush it away.'

'Oh—where?' I sat up abruptly. With infinite care Coco removed the insect from my left breast because, as he pointed out, if it were brushed away it might get squashed and that would leave a mark.

'I do hope it hasn't stained the material,' he said. 'I

tried to take it off carefully. When you get home you'd better just sponge it lightly with a damp cloth to make sure.'

'Oh, it doesn't matter,' I said crossly. The afternoon was coming to an end and the illusion of getting away from it all by having lunch in the country with Coco could not be sustained indefinitely and soon I should have to face Alan again.

'Shall we go back?' I suggested.

Coco rose to his feet with rather too much alacrity.

'Yes, let's,' he agreed, handing me solicitously along the path through the woods and back to the car. Perhaps the afternoon had been a disappointment to him; the promise of my arrival at Dolly's in distress had hardly been fulfilled. It had been disappointing for me, too, though I had expected less. It was my own fault for thinking that Coco could do anything for me in such a situation.

As we drove back I imagined myself in London staying with my sister, being made much of by the sort of person I could not at this moment visualise.

'Have you thought of divorcing him?' Coco asked. 'That would be the best thing, wouldn't it?'

I must have looked startled, for the idea of divorce had never entered my mind, and Coco went on to talk about the difficulty of keeping up a façade, of pretending that things were all right when they weren't.

'Even Mother had difficulties of that kind,' he confided. 'A beautiful woman like Mother!' he said, as if emphasising the difference between us. 'And it was worse for her because some of the women were black.'

'Would that make it worse? Yes, I suppose on the island it might. Here it would hardly make any difference.'

'But it would make a *little* difference, wouldn't it, Caro? Even you and Alan, liberal-minded and anti-racist as you are, must feel that.'

I was confused and now began to wonder if the girl Alan had told me about had been black. And whether it would have made any difference.

'Caro, you cannot live a lie,' Coco was saying. 'It wouldn't be like you to live a lie. *I* think you should go to your mother for a while. That is the place for you to be.'

'You don't know my mother,' I protested. Yet I did feel that there was something in what he said. The idea of going to stay with my mother was more attractive than taking my humiliation to Susan in London, and by the time I had reached home I had decided on a definite course of action. I would take Kate with me, Inge would go back to Sweden for her holiday and Alan would be alone to do as he pleased. In a week or two things might have resolved themselves one way or the other.

XV

Married when leaves in October thin
Toil and hardships for you begin . . .

I couldn't help thinking of
the old rhyme as I sat in the train with Kate on the way
to my mother's. Not that anybody had actually gone so
far as to say it, even in a joke, but there had been a
feeling in the air that I could have done better for myself.
My mother had found it hard to conceal her disappointment over David, the rising young politician, the ideal
son-in-law. Yet Alan, in his way, had been just as am-

bitious and now one could say that he had done as well as David, only in a different field.

'How are your students?' my mother asked warily as we went to the car in the station yard. She had not yet brought herself to ask after Alan. I was able to tell her that they seemed to be quiet at the moment.

Then Kate piped up with something about Daddy, or rather Daddy's car. It had something that Granny's hadn't got and that diverted us for a while, but of course it led us on to Alan and I had to bring out the carefully prepared story of how we had thought it might be good to have separate holidays this year, which *lots* of people did. Really, it gave me a chance to stay with her just with Kate—there was never really room at the cottage for the three of us—and it would be *lovely*. This gorgeous *weather*, how I hoped it would last. And I might even go and spend a few days with Susan in London if I could leave Kate.

My mother seemed enthusiastic. 'Kate stay with Granny,' she declared. Kate looked up at me frowning. I changed the subject hastily.

My mother had moved into the cottage after my father's death when I had already left home, so it had no girlhood memories. There was no danger of being put to sleep in my old room or of finding favourite toys in a cupboard. The spare room had two divan beds and no feeling of anybody having lived or suffered in it, crying into the pillow, laughing or loving. And yet it was an old cottage—people must have been born and perhaps even died in this room but they had vanished without trace.

'The bed by the window is a little wider, so I thought that one for you,' my mother was saying.

I looked around me with pleasure, knowing that

there would be everything I could possibly want or need
and some things that I would never have thought of in
the room. Having people to stay was one of the main
interests of my mother's life and now she did it very
well. Only the presence of Kate might take something
from the gracious comfort of my surroundings. Already
she had found the tin of biscuits on the small table between the beds and was trying to prise off the lid with
cries of 'Bicky, bicky.'

'What heaven it will be when she's a bit older and
we can have proper conversation,' I observed.

'You haven't ever thought . . .' my mother began.

'Of having another one. Well, I suppose we might
one day.' But that day now seemed remoter than ever.
I remembered Susan that morning at Easter, sitting on
the council's wooden seat and telling me about her abortion in Kilburn and I suddenly felt sorry for my mother
who had been kept out of it all.

'Well, there's a drink downstairs when you're ready,'
my mother said briskly. 'When does Kate like to have
her supper?'

When we had disposed of Kate, bathed her and put
her to bed and hidden the biscuit tin, we were able to
settle down with our drinks with the secure feeling of
there being something in the oven that wouldn't spoil.
It was the time for confidences but all I could think of
to say—and I suppose it was a confidence in a way—
was 'Who do you think I had lunch with a few weeks
ago?'

'David?' my mother queried in an almost hopeful
tone as if even now something might come of it.

'Yes. I ran into him as I was coming out of a church
where I'd been to a memorial service. We had a very
cosy lunch together.'

'And he still hasn't married?'

'No. I suppose he hasn't found anybody suitable yet.'

'Such a *pity* . . .' My mother seemed unable to go on. 'You know, this sort of thing must happen quite often. So many women have to put up with second best so I suppose I hoped that you and Susan would do better than I did.'

I looked at her in amazement. My father had been an ordinary, not particularly interesting sort of man, but I had never realised, as my mother seemed now to imply, that he had been second best. I was embarrassed and didn't know what to say. Luckily my mother helped me out.

'Oh, yes,' she said calmly. 'I was in love with somebody else when I married your father.'

'Who was it? Not anybody I *know*, surely?'

She smiled a rather complacent little smile. 'Not personally, perhaps, but you'll have seen him often on television.'

She named a rather good-looking outspoken clergyman who often appeared—without his clerical collar—on programmes of a controversial nature.

I was astonished and she was pleased at this. Again, I couldn't think what to say. I could see that she was drawing a parallel between herself and this man and me and David. She might have been the wife of a television personality, I of a Member of Parliament. As it was, she was the widow of a bank manager and I the wife of a lecturer in a provincial university.

'Well,' I said at last, 'I suppose that's life, isn't it?'

At this she got up and went into the kitchen to get the supper and I sat meditating on this same aspect of life, my perceptions a little blurred by drink so that I saw myself at one moment rushing back to Alan, and making it up in a wonderful scene, and the next, seeking out David and offering myself to him. But how, exactly? I didn't even know where he lived.

Waking the next morning I had a moment of panic, forgetting where I was and unable to recognise any familiar object in the strange room. Then Kate called out and I remembered. Hours and days, perhaps even weeks stretched before me, all blank. How was I going to fill them?

After breakfast we went shopping, then had coffee at the Old Forge. Two women who had just retired from jobs in London came to lunch. They were rather nice, spinster sisters, one in her late fifties and the other just sixty. Their lives were busy in an admirable way, full of interest and the pleasure of having time to do the things they had always wanted to do. I regarded them with envy as they described alterations they were making to their garden and the motoring holiday in Shropshire they had planned for later in the year. They were still good-looking and one of them, I felt sure, had once been beautiful. They must have loved in their time, perhaps loved and lost and come through it unscathed.

After tea my mother explained apologetically that it was her week to do the flowers in church but that I needn't come along if I didn't want to—perhaps Kate would like to help? It seemed a way of passing the time so I went, too, my arms full of delphiniums and irises and branches of young green beech leaves. We went into the church and removed the old flowers which were already shedding their petals on the stone floor. Like most non-churchgoers I felt a certain inhibition and indefinable fear when I was inside the building, lowering my voice and restraining Kate from running about and exploring. My mother, who had not been much of a churchgoer either until she went to live in the village, seemed much more at home, bustling about with the sheaves of flowers and branches which she began to put in the vases in the same sort of floral arrangement style I had noticed at Esther Clovis's memorial service. Kate was happily occupied, stroking a little marble dog she had discovered on a tomb, lying at the feet of its master. I, with my lack of artistic talent, could only offer to fill the jugs and vases, which meant going round to the tap at the back of the church.

There was a sort of no-man's-land of long grass, nettles and dock leaves with a shed whose open door revealed old vases and chipped pottery jugs and a green metal contraption for holding flowers on graves. There were also a few decayed red hassocks with the stuffing coming out and what appeared to be an old, though hardly antique, religious statue, a sickly painted representation of some unrecognised-by-me saint. I filled the vases at the tap and was carrying them away when I thought I heard a movement in the long grass beyond me. I stopped and peered, then realised that it was a couple of lovers, so I hurried past with averted eyes in the way one does. There was something upsetting about the sight with all its significance for me. Back in the church I tried to arrange the branches of beech, which were intractable and refused to go the way we wanted them to.

'Can I help?' said a man's voice. Somebody I took to be the vicar was standing beside us.

For a moment I thought of taking his offer at its face value, as if he were a marriage guidance counsellor, and asking him to help me make it up with Alan. But

of course it was unfair of me to expect that he had meant
anything more than to hold the beech branches while I
tried to arrange the flowers around them. He was a
rather distinguished-looking man of about sixty, obviously greatly at ease in the presence of women. On
the way home I asked my mother about him, but she
only grumbled about his having introduced something
called Series One or Series Two, I forget which, when
everyone in the village preferred the service to be left
as it was. How narrow our lives become, I thought, and
although I was half my mother's age I could feel mine
becoming narrower too.

That evening the telephone rang. I hoped it might
be Alan, but it was Coco. He did so wonder—and Kitty
had of course been wondering, too—how things were
going for me. It had been such a good thing for me to
go and stay with my mother, they both thought, but
of course he was longing for me to come back. The
weather had been quite hot and Kitty had worn her
white dress to go to a garden party in a nearby village.
It was so seldom that one could wear white in England.

I stood with the receiver in my hand, holding it
away from my ear as Coco's voice went on.

'I helped to do the flowers in church,' I said, 'and
met the vicar.'

'Is there anything I can do?' he asked hopefully.

'No, thank you, Coco,' I said firmly. 'It was very
sweet of you to take me out to lunch that day when I
asked you.'

'It was my pleasure.' Coco's tone became anxious.
'I only hope that insect didn't mark your gown. Such
an annoying thing to happen. Mother sends her love
and of course Dolly does, too. Take care of yourself.'

My mother wondered aloud who had telephoned

and as I felt unable to explain Coco she assumed it was a girlfriend. That did not seem entirely inappropriate so I let it be.

The next morning I accompanied my mother to church and it seemed a good chance to take Kate. Like most liberal-minded people of my generation I was all for children being given the opportunity to follow whatever religion appealed to them, though I was guiltily aware that neither Alan nor I had done much about it so far. Still, she was young and had not yet started to ask questions. I had told her that the dead birds and shrews we had buried and Dolly's hedgehog had all gone to sleep in the earth and that had seemed to satisfy her. But was it good enough? I asked myself anxiously as we sat in church. Might it not even be wrong and harmful? Perhaps Kate's mind was not yet fully enquiring but it was too much to expect that she would always accept whatever I told her.

In church she sat silent, obviously fascinated by the goings-on up at the altar, for it was a high church and the vicar had three servers assisting him. I thought it was 'interesting' and wished I could feel something. I attended to the prayers and was startled at the words 'enlighten with thy spirit all places of education and learning', seeing my own university with its undenominational meeting-house, the dead pigeon lying in the water and the obscenity scrawled on the piece of modern sculpture. One would have thought that enlightenment could hardly go further than that.

XVI

My sister, Susan, gloried in the squalor of the neighbourhood where she lived—the peeling stucco or garishly painted houses, the street markets with yams and green bananas on the stalls, the nights disturbed by loud music and noisy quarrels. It was teeming with life—black, brown, yellow and white—and offered all the problems that interested her—race relations, bad housing, the Irish question, teenage unmarried mothers, mixed marriages and many more.

'If only you and Alan weren't so *civilised* . . .' she lamented. 'If only you'd shout and throw things and then tumble into bed and make it up. You're so cold and English and provincial—afraid the au pair girl might hear, or the neighbours!'

We were in a bus going along the Harrow Road. I sat narrowly on the edge of the seat, three-quarters of which was taken up by a large, jolly West Indian dressed entirely in pale turquoise blue. 'And Negro ladies in white muslin gowns,' I thought, wondering where the line had come from. Susan was in front of me and I wished she wouldn't talk so freely about my private affairs, throwing back advice in her loud clear voice for all the bus to hear, though I had to admit that nobody seemed to be taking the slightest bit of notice.

'Alan and I aren't *like* that,' I protested in a lower tone. 'Not that we're all that civilised or care about the neighbours, but it just wouldn't be like us to shout and throw things.'

I hadn't meant to tell her much about me and Alan but of course in the end it had all come out, even the details like the milk boiling over that morning, Iris Horniblow and the artificial rose, and the ludicrous incident of my lunch with Coco and the insect on my 'gown'. I was more cagey about Cressida but eventually I told Susan about her too and she nodded and smiled in a satisfied sort of way as the details of Alan's infidelity were unfolded. She had been expecting—perhaps even hoping—that something of the kind might happen.

'After all, you've been married about seven years,' she pointed out. 'It's a wonder nothing like this has happened before, or has it?'

'I don't know. Perhaps it has.'

'Are you going to see this Cressida—contrive a meeting or something?'

'I don't know. What good would it do?'

'None at all, but aren't you curious?'

'In a way, but I think I'd rather it was like one of

those novels where people *don't* meet—you know, the novelist carefully not bringing them together.'

'That might be because the novelist can't think how to make them behave and so takes the easy way out.'

Back at Susan's flat, Gary Carter, the television designer she lived with, came in and we couldn't talk about my problems any more. He did not seem to have much to say and obviously thought me boring and provincial. I sat dumbly unable to think of any conversational gambit except 'What have you been designing lately?' and that was so feeble I didn't even attempt it. At last he went into the kitchen and came out again with a glass of milk and I made a mental note that he was that kind of person. It seemed obvious that the only thing to do now was to go to bed, so he and Susan retired to their room, Susan coming out at intervals to ask if I'd like a bath or to help me arrange the bedclothes on the bed-settee.

Eventually I got into bed, feeling strange as one always does sleeping in the middle of somebody's sitting room. I wondered about Gary and Susan, whether they felt my presence in the flat inhibiting, but after some mumbled conversation there was silence from their room and I was left alone and wide awake, as I thought. Yet the next thing I knew was that Susan was standing over me with a mug of coffee and it was morning.

That evening Susan and Gary were giving 'a sort of party'. The sitting room, dimly lit, looked like a purple and green cave, with posters stuck on the walls and the dullness of the textbooks and sociology paperbacks transformed by the rosy glow of the dimmed lights. None of the people—and there seemed to be a great many of them—had any clear identity for me. There was none of that business of feeling obliged to talk to elderly professors' wives or finding oneself stuck in a corner with a boring young lecturer who could only talk his own particular shop. And yet in its way this party was no less tedious than some of the university gatherings, I thought, as an unattractive bearded face pushed itself rather too close. As the evening went on somebody felt, and was, sick and the people living over the road complained about the noise.

A few hours later, in bed in the middle of the sitting room, but this time surrounded by fumes of cigarette smoke and the smell of drink and the debris we'd been too tired to clear away, it was hardly surprising that sleep did not come as easily as the night before. My mouth was sore from too much smoking and my stomach slightly queasy from the unwise mixture of food and drink. As I lay awake I could hear Gary snoring in the room next door and I wondered if Susan was lying awake beside him. I propped myself up on one elbow and took a sip of water and two aspirins.

I wondered what Alan was doing, imagined him in the empty house, not yet gone to bed, perhaps still reading his proofs, brooding over Cressida and the diagram. I knew that I must go and see her; my curiosity would drive me to it. Then I thought of Crispin Maynard in Italy reading Alan's article and I wondered how he would react to it. We must see that Alan sent offprints to the right people—that was most important.

Next I began wondering about Mr. Stillingfleet's manuscript, trying to remember where I had put it. For some reason—but I suppose being awake in the middle of the night when one is liable to worry was reason enough—I found myself anxiously going over all that had happened at Normanhurst. What exactly had we done, Alan and I? Mr. Stillingfleet was dead now and there were no relations, so what was there to worry about? Crispin Maynard had evidently never seen the manuscript—though he suspected its existence—nor had Sister Dew; not even Evan Cranton, who had the rest of Mr. Stillingfleet's papers in the library, would realise that anything was missing. Or would he? Supposing there had been a list or inventory of what was in the box? That would show exactly what was supposed to be there and somebody reading Alan's article would know that he must have taken that particular manuscript. Surely people didn't think about that sort of thing when they read an article in a learned journal, I told myself. Yet I knew that sometimes they did. I remembered Iris Horniblow and her question to Alan about how one cited unpublished stuff that one wasn't supposed to have seen. Why had Alan and I not discussed this possibility? Why had we not taken steps to return the manuscript as soon as he had finished with it? My mind was becoming more and more confused as these half-thoughts chased each other round and round. Was it my responsibility? Alan had left it to me—but that did not seem fair. I sat up and drank some more water. It seemed that the only way we could get the manuscript back with the other papers was for me to get a job in the library. Dawn was breaking and I realised that birds start singing early even in London. As I listened to their chorus I saw the face of Evan Cranton. It was not a face I was used to conjuring up, as one sometimes tries to conjure up the face of a lover. On the contrary: it came to me clearly and its expression was sarcastic.

XVII

Things being as they were, I suppose it was only to be expected that I should feel a deep sense of inferiority as I made my way to the editorial offices of Rollo Gaunt's journal. Furthermore, I was not sure where to get off the bus—it was somewhere in Gray's Inn Road—and in my uncertainty I nearly missed my stop. The bus was starting up again and I almost fell into the arms of a good-looking, solid, barrister type carrying a sort of dark red laundry bag embroidered with initials. He steadied me on the pavement with a smile and directed me towards the street I was looking for. The encounter made me feel a little better. I walked more purposefully and began to go over what I could say when I met 'Cressida'. I couldn't think of her as a real person. I supposed I might pretend that I had come on some sort of business connected with the journal. It then occurred to me that she might not be alone. I would have to play it by ear.

I had arrived at the correct address—Wormwood Mews—but it seemed a most unlikely place for a learned journal to have its editorial offices. All the numbers, which went from side to side with the odd A or B thrown in for confusion, indicated garages or mews cottages or studios. I walked up and down peering. Then I came upon a small house with the journal's brass name-plate on the doorway and what looked like a flat on the top storey. Cressida obviously lived over the office and so, once the editorial business was settled, what could be easier or more cosy, I thought sourly, than to pop upstairs to Cressida's flat? I tried to picture all the academics I knew who had published articles in Rollo Gaunt's journal doing such a thing, but it seemed unlikely. I tapped on the front door. It was open, so I pushed it and went in.

A scene of chaos met my eyes. A large table was covered with piles of books, typescripts and galley proofs, some of which had slipped to the floor. Trails of printed labels were festooned over chairs and hanging from bookcases and bulldog clips on the back of the door. In the middle of it all, acting out the cliché of 'wringing her hands', stood a tall blonde girl with a rather horsey, well-bred face and untidy hair like a lion's mane.

'Universal Aunts or Brook Street Bureau?' she asked hopefully.

'Neither, I'm afraid. But perhaps,' I found myself saying, 'I could help you tidy things up a bit.'

My tone must have sounded as doubtful as I felt, for helping Cressida to tidy her office was not exactly the purpose of my visit. 'I'm Caroline Grimstone,' I added.

'Oh, golly, Dr. Grimstone's diagram!' was her re-action. Unlikely as it might seem, this appeared to be the only connection in which she thought of him. 'Is he still cross with me for making a balls-up of it?'

'I don't know,' I said. 'I don't think so.'

Cressida sat down with exaggerated heaviness. She seemed something of a comic character, not at all what I had expected. This made me see things differently. I imagined Alan coming to this chaotic office, losing his temper with her because of her stupidity over the dia-gram and Cressida bursting into tears. I felt sure that she was the sort of girl who cried easily. Then what? Alan putting his arms round her to comfort her and so, eventually, upstairs to her flat. Or perhaps they had lunch together and things had happened afterwards— that was more likely.

'What can I do for you, then?' she asked. 'If you've come to get Dr. Grimstone's offprints I'm afraid they won't be ready for ages yet.'

'Yes.' It seemed easier to accept her reason for my visit, for it was beginning to dawn on me that Cressida and I weren't going to have any sort of showdown of the kind I had imagined. I could see her now as a jolly friendly girl who would go to bed with anyone and think nothing of it; perhaps Alan had taken her too seriously and I had, too.

'Would you like some coffee?'

'Thanks.'

She unearthed a couple of mugs from the muddle on the table and put the kettle on. As we were drinking the coffee there was a knock on the door and the girl from Universal Aunts or perhaps Brook Street Bureau arrived and I seized the opportunity to slip away as Cressida was giving her rather muddled explanations and instructions. The opportunity of having it out with Cressida was lost forever. If I couldn't discuss things with her I should be able to do so now with Alan. I decided to go home as soon as I had collected Kate.

XVIII

'Caro, thank goodness you're back!'

Alan had, it seemed, been waiting at the station for a full half hour before the train was due. I put Kate into the back of the car and allowed myself to bask for a moment in the luxury of having been missed while Alan put the suitcases into the boot.

'I phoned you last night, but your mother said you'd gone to Susan's. I didn't know what to do.'

I smiled at him fondly.

'It's Crispin,' he said. 'He's read the proofs after all and he's making trouble with Rollo Gaunt over my article. Now he wants Rollo to hold up publication while he writes a rebuttal.'

'But you gave him the chance to read it before,' I said.

'That's what I told Rollo—anyway, it's too late now to stop publication. I think the proofs have already gone back to the printer.'

I thought of the chaos of that editorial office and wondered if this was so, but of course I did not say anything.

'Too late,' echoed Kate from the back of the car, and we were home.

After I had unpacked and was putting things away in drawers I came upon Mr. Stillingfleet's manuscript and began leafing through it, but most of it consisted of extracts from African stories and proverbs in some strange dialect with odd letters and symbols, so I could make nothing of it. This, then, was what Crispin had wanted and it must have been a shock to him to discover that Alan had somehow managed to get hold of it. I imagined him at his villa, perhaps doing nothing the first few days but resting and enjoying the sun, then feeling the need to read something and going to his briefcase where Margaret had packed one or two journals, offprints, proofs—the sort of thing that academics send to each other—and thinking, Oh yes, young Grimstone's article, I might read that now. This was easy to picture, but what I couldn't understand was the nastiness of his action in making a fuss to Rollo Gaunt. It didn't seem like Crispin, so noble and kind and helpful, so anxious, I would have said, to encourage a younger scholar, even in his own field. I said as much to Alan and was surprised to learn that he had never had this high opinion of Crispin as a person that I thought was shared by everyone.

'Just because he's nice to you and is old and on the

point of retiring doesn't necessarily mean that he has all those splendid qualities you credit him with. He wanted to get hold of that manuscript and he's livid to think that I've succeeded where he failed—it's as simple as that.'

'*You* didn't exactly succeed,' I pointed out.

'Caro, I had to do what I did. But you do see that I need your help now to replace the manuscript?'

'Couldn't we just burn it?' I asked.

'Caro!' Alan looked really shocked, as if I had suggested murder. 'It is vital material and must be available for other scholars now.' I was interested to observe that his scruples were academic rather than moral. 'No, it has to go back to the library with the other Stillingfleet papers. You must help!'

'All right,' I said, doubtfully. 'I'll try.'

'You must catch Dr. Cranton at an unguarded moment,' said Coco, but somehow I couldn't imagine that there ever were any such moments in his life, certainly not in the library. I had not of course told Coco what I wanted to do; I had implied that I wanted to get something from the library that wasn't easily accessible. His curiosity was aroused but he was too indolent to press me for details, and he and Kitty were suggesting ways in which this might be done.

It was one of those evenings when after a hot day it is possible to sit under the trees in an English garden, enjoying the shade and anticipating the approach of night almost as if one were in a tropical climate. Kitty was at her best at such times in her filmy, romantic-looking dresses; the failing light was kind and it was difficult to believe that she was over sixty or even that Coco was over forty.

'Dr. Cranton might fall in love with you,' said Coco idly.

'Oh, you always think of that as a solution,' I said impatiently.

'A common interest in something *might* lead to love,' said Kitty, but she sounded as if she considered it extremely unlikely. Obviously there had been no nonsense about interests in common with the men who had loved *her*. 'But I don't think I could be interested in a lot of old manuscripts,' she went on. 'Dust always gives me sinusitis and I shouldn't care to handle them at *all*. You don't know *where* they've been.'

'Well, Mother, you will never have to,' said Coco.

'I can't think why women want to do such things,' said Kitty, 'unless they need the money, of course.'

I thought of saying something about the satisfaction of working, but when I came to think of it I wasn't at all sure that a job in the library would bring that kind of fulfilment and anyway I didn't know yet whether Evan Cranton would be willing to employ me.

XIX

Dr. Cranton—he was very much Dr. at that moment—smiled in a tigerish way.

'A nice little job for the mornings, is that what you want? Something to take you away from the kitchen sink?'

'That seems to be a negative way of putting it,' I ventured, bold in my nervousness. Why couldn't Alan see how frightening he was? 'I'd like to do something useful, and Heather—Mrs. Armitage—thought . . .'

'Oh, she thought, did she? Mrs. Armitage thought. That you might help her with her crushing load, take some of the weight off her shoulders?'

'She didn't put it like that, but it seems the work's increasing.'

'Oh, yes, work is always increasing. Parkinson's Law operates as well in university libraries as anywhere else.'

'I suppose it does. Perhaps there isn't a job for me then.' I felt dejected and must have shown it, for Dr. Cranton suddenly relented and became almost as he had been at the Dabbs Memorial Lecture.

'My dear, I didn't say that. The only difficulty is that there will be one extra for *coffee* in the mornings—I wonder how they will cope with *that*!' The thought seemed to please him and he was suddenly genial. Practical arrangements were discussed, then he handed me over to Heather. 'Mrs. Armitage will show you what to do.'

Heather waited until he was well out of earshot, then said, 'Of course, there isn't much I can give you to do at the *moment*, since you are inexperienced, and what there is will seem rather menial. Let me see now . . .' She moved her hands among the papers and cards on her table, enjoying the importance of her position. I stood there expectantly, wondering if there would be anywhere for me to sit and what, if anything, she would find me to do.

'I know,' she said. 'You can stick the labels on the backs of these books. They've all been written out, all you have to do is stick them on. You can use a corner of that table there.'

'Thank you,' I said humbly, pushing a pile of books aside, or rather not pushing them exactly, but moving them six inches to the right so that I should have a little space to work. This was the kind of thing that Kate could do. She was already making good progress in composing pictures of gummed paper shapes and showed a sense of colour and form that Alan and I found remarkable. I stuck on one of the labels, slightly crooked. No doubt I would soon progress to more responsible work. Then I would have a chance to find out where the manuscript Africana were kept and put back Mr. Stillingfleet's manuscript.

Summer began to move towards autumn and the September mornings were cool and bright. There was even a touch of frost in the air. It seemed a time for looking forward and perhaps even for making resolutions to alter and improve one's life. The beginning of the new academic year was the most suitable time for us to think of changes and we knew that some would be forced upon us.

In the meantime Alan had received a letter from Rollo Gaunt saying that he had not seen any necessity to hold up Alan's article to await Crispin's reply. 'After all, I *am* the editor,' he had said when he and Alan talked it over. Both had come to the conclusion that Crispin was getting past it. Alan suggested also that this kind of academic controversy was old-fashioned, almost Victorian, the kind of thing that was amusing to read about but was quite irrelevant and out of place nowadays. It was a waste of time and clouded the issue, the business of who got what from where. It wasn't as if there was any question of plagiarism—hadn't there been a novel about an affair of this kind where somebody stole somebody else's diagram and used it in a thesis? Ah, yes, Rollo remembered a very good play on that very topic on the London stage some years ago. He had gone with his mother and Lisa—his first wife, that was—and *her* mother and father. It had been a most successful evening and afterwards they had gone to that delightful French restaurant, Chez something or other, where they had eaten a memorable asparagus mousse. So Alan, reporting this conversation to me later, had as it were pulled the wool over Rollo's eyes and distracted him from the main question. Alan began to prepare another article on a different aspect of the subject and we waited confidently for the new term to begin. I went on guarding the manuscript, still waiting for an opportunity to slip it back, but quite often forgetting about it altogether, for there were other matters to occupy me.

This term had brought new and more assertive students and two lecturers, fresh from the London School of Economics with revolutionary ideas about the way things should be organised.

'They seem to want to do away with everything,' I said to Dolly as I sat in her garden watching her collect a little pile of hedgehog droppings for some unknown purpose.

'A good thing, too,' she said stoutly, and I could tell that she was in one of her irritating moods when out of cussedness she would disagree with whatever one said.

'All that academic pomp and ceremony is out of place these days. I should have thought you would feel that, Caro. After all, you are a good forty years younger than I am.'

'But they want the students to decide on their own courses and what books they should read—and to abolish written work and exams . . .' I faltered. 'Alan would be out of a job if they had their way.'

'No one was ever the better for having passed a written examination,' Dolly stated. 'There, look at that.' She indicated the neat pile of black droppings.

'What use are *they*?' I asked meanly.

'Oh, what does it matter what *use* they are! It's enough to see such tangible evidence of another kind of life!'

I could see that she was about to embark on her favourite topic of Nature and the study of animals in their natural habitat and the benefit this could bring, so I tried to turn the conversation. She began to talk about the old people at Normanhurst and how Sister Dew would be grateful if I would go on reading aloud to them this autumn.

'Well, I'm working in the library in the mornings,' I said, 'so I'll be rather busy,' for I felt that I had done my share of reading aloud. The trouble with doing good works is that one can never be said to have done one's share because some works always need doing and there are never enough people to do them.

'And what exactly are you *doing* in the library?' Dolly asked quite kindly.

'Oh, I'm making card indexes now and sorting papers—you've no idea what a lot of stuff there is,' I said, conscious that it all sounded totally inessential.

'I'm sure it will be very useful to Dr. Cranton,' said Dolly, 'but will it really occupy your mind and heart? Is it really worthy of you? Will it fulfill any deep need?'

I pondered on this as I walked home. I thought I would call in to see Iris Horniblow who could be my friend now that I knew that Alan did not love her. I stood on her doorstep, rang the bell of her flat and waited, but there was no reply and I was just about to give up and go away when Iris came down the stairs. She was wearing pink trousers and smelt very strongly of expensive scent, perhaps excessively so for the middle of the afternoon. Then I noticed for the first time a red car parked outside the house and I recognised it as belonging to one of the new young lecturers.

'Oh, hullo, Caro,' she said. 'Come in.'

I hesitated, for I was conscious of having interrupted something. 'I was just passing . . .' I said.

For some reason Iris seemed anxious that I should go in and when I walked into the sitting room I thought I saw why. The new lecturer, a dark, good-looking young man with shoulder-length wavy hair, was making tea and obviously knew exactly where everything was kept. It was natural and rather touching that Iris should want to show off her new lover, so much more personable than Alan. There was a warmth and domesticity about the scene. Iris introduced me and I recalled Alan had mentioned meeting Ian Ashton. He spoke rather reverently about Alan as if he were of a much older generation and I realised that Ian was very young, not more than twenty-four or -five, so that one could almost say that Iris was cradle-snatching. This gave me an obscure feeling of satisfaction and I pitied her, seeing the end of the affair before she did. There was a kind of hardness and ruthlessness about Ian for all his youth, and I wondered if it would be he who would incite the students to revolution and what form the rebellion would take.

XX

The appearance of Alan's article coincided suitably enough, I felt, with the return of Crispin and Margaret from Italy. It seemed that while Alan was now consolidating his position as the leader of the new young school of ethno-historians, Crispin was moving into a graceful retirement. I would have liked to think of him casting off his mantle so that it fell onto Alan's shoulders in a manner that was both natural and appropriate, but I knew that this was a naive and sentimental way of looking at things.

'I'm glad that Rollo went ahead with your article and didn't wait for Crispin's counter-attack,' I said to Alan. 'It was obviously the best thing to do, and I expect

Crispin will forget all about it now and look forward to the presentation of his portrait.'

Alan seemed to think this likely, or at least he agreed with me, but rather in the way of one who is tired of a subject and doesn't want to think any more about it. His mind was now on something else and as the term went on there was a repetition of the pattern in which he retired to his study in the evenings and I lay awake hearing the tapping of his typewriter and wishing he would come to bed.

I had taken to carrying Mr. Stillingfleet's manuscript about with me in my shopping bag, waiting for an opportunity to slip it back with the rest of his papers. This was not easy because they were kept in Dr. Cranton's private office. He was said to be going to do something about them but nobody knew exactly what. As Mr. Stillingfleet had left no provision for their disposal in his will it was felt that no immediate action was necessary.

One morning, however, I had my chance. Evan Cranton did not come in at his usual time of half-past nine and about a quarter to eleven a message came from Menna Cranton. He had a heavy cold and she had decided to 'keep him in'. There was an immediate lightening of the atmosphere, a sad reflection on some of us part-time graduate wives striving to fulfil ourselves with useful work. Somebody took out a copy of the *Daily Express*, another, more self-righteously, the *Guardian*, a third *The Times* crossword. I got up from my table and went in the direction of the cloakroom carrying my shopping bag, but, when nobody was looking, I slipped into Dr. Cranton's office.

This was a small, rather dark room facing north;

the only thing to be said in its favour was that it was private. Most of the space was taken up with a heavy desk and there was a block of filing cabinets against one wall. Menna Cranton had made a cushion for her husband's chair out of some left-over Jacobean chintz curtain material. The desk was tidy and there were only a few things in the in-tray. I felt very nervous and disliked the idea of looking in the drawers of the desk which rather to my surprise did not seem to be locked. I think I was afraid of finding something that would embarrass me or give me an insight into Dr. Cranton's private life that I would rather not have had. But the top drawer contained only a pipe, a packet of pipe-cleaners and a number of old notebooks and diaries. Curious, I opened one of the diaries—1965—and saw that it was almost empty. 'SCOLMA comm. meeting 2.30', I read for one day, but it meant nothing to me. The other drawers were equally unrevealing, except that one labelled 'Bibliography' contained nothing but empty notebooks and packets of new cards. Perhaps this was the work he was saving for his retirement.

The filing cabinets were locked and I thought they might contain personal files relating to the staff. I didn't feel that the Stillingfleet papers were likely to be in them so I turned my attention to a large cupboard, fortunately unlocked.

My first feeling was one of dismay for its shelves were crammed with files and bundles of paper. It wouldn't be much use replacing the manuscript if I couldn't put it back in the right place.

'Oh, Caroline, *there* you are . . .'

I was horribly startled until I saw that it was only Heather Armitage. She was carrying two mugs and I realised that of course it must be coffee time, that moment for which one was never too absorbed in one's work to break off.

'I was afraid that your coffee would get cold,' she said fussily. 'Do you want it here?'

'I don't know,' I said, flustered. 'Perhaps I ought not to drink it *here*.'

'Well, if Dr. Cranton gives you work to do that makes it necessary for you to be in his office he can hardly object to you drinking your coffee here,' she said, evidently in one of her anti-librarian moods.

'Quite,' I said.

We sat down and Heather offered me a cigarette. There was an air of defiance about our action—almost a feeling of women's liberation in the air.

'I think it's a bit much to expect you to do tidying-up jobs,' Heather went on. 'After all, you're a graduate.' Tidying up was obviously more menial than sticking on labels.

'Yes, but I only work part-time,' I mumbled.

'Just look at the mess in this cupboard!'

'Yes, I must admit I was surprised,' I said smugly. 'Dr. Cranton always seems to be such a tidy person.'

'All this has obviously been swept under the carpet,' said Heather, making an extravagant gesture. 'What *is* it, anyway? Have you looked at it?'

'I think it's supposed to be manuscript sources in African history,' I said, for I could see now that the bottom shelf was labelled 'Stillingfleet'.

'Oh, all ready for his great work of classification,' said Heather scornfully. 'And what's all *this* . . . ?'

While her back was turned and she was trying to pull open the drawer of a filing cabinet I slipped the manuscript in among the Stillingfleet papers.

'What are you two doing in the librarian's office?' One of the male library assistants stood in the doorway.

'Just sorting things out,' said Heather in a rather belligerent tone.

'One of those things that women think they do so much better than men,' he said, teasing us.

'We don't *think* about whether we do things better than men,' Heather retorted. 'We just go ahead and do them!'

The real purpose of our being in the office or the possibility of our presence being questioned or enquired into was mercifully lost in this jocular man-woman exchange.

'What's *this*?' the library assistant asked, bringing himself down to our level by his curiosity. 'Good heavens, it's all that Africana. So that's what he's done with it. Did you ever see such a mess!'

He was rather an old-womanish young man and the three of us tut-tutted and chatted cosily about the state the papers were in without making the slightest attempt to tidy them up.

XXI

'Another glass of sherry?' Alan looked at me doubtfully, then at his watch. 'They won't be here for half an hour yet.'

'And you want me to be sober enough to cope, naturally. But you realise that I *need* drink to give me courage to face people like Iris and Ian Ashton.'

'Maybe—but oughtn't you to be in the kitchen fussing over something?'

'Inge's done most of it. Then she's taking Kate with Luke and Alice to Iris's sister.' She was a married childless woman, who was said to 'adore' children and who looked after Iris's two whenever she got the opportunity, which was quite often.

'Then we'll have a nice grown-up lunch,' said Alan.

'That was the general idea.'

We were sitting in Alan's study, which was at the
back of the house and got the sun. He had arranged
drinks in here, not necessarily, I felt, because it was the
warmest and brightest room, but in order to present
himself in his natural setting and one which was as becoming to him as a jungle background was to an exotic
bird or agile furry animal. Instead of a desk he had a
heavy table on which were set out wire filing baskets,
notebooks and card indexes; a neatly folded bundle of
galley proofs had either been or was about to be corrected, while a sheet of paper in the typewriter gave a
hint of work in progress. The carefully arranged tray of
coloured biros and newly sharpened pencils looked almost too perfect, if one had not known that Alan was
a naturally tidy person whose working tools were always in meticulous order. The small bookcase behind
the table held reference books and runs of journals rel-
evant to his field.

A smaller table with a different air about it, with
drinks and a few chairs ranged round it, had been placed
in the window and it was here that he and I were sitting,
enjoying the sun, the effect of the sherry taking from
us any sense of urgency or stress. There was a red Vir-
ginia creeper framing the window and beyond that a
glimpse of late roses and Michaelmas daisies.

I lay back in my chair and cast a sideways look at
Alan almost as if I were flirting with somebody I was
meeting for the first time. He returned my glance in the
same spirit, but our mutual regard was interrupted by
the sudden appearance at the window of a man's face,
with a slightly startled expression, round eyes peering
behind spectacles, longish curly hair and sidewhiskers.

'Who is it?' I asked, almost in fear.

'Rollo Gaunt,' said Alan, obviously puzzled. 'I know I told him to drop in any time he was in this part of the world, but I never thought . . .'

The sort of invitation, I thought, that an author who has just had a paper accepted by a learned journal might very well throw out to the editor in an impulse of gratitude and euphoria.

Alan had gone to the door and returned bringing with him Rollo Gaunt, who apologised for the unusual way he had made his appearance.

'Looking in at people's windows,' he said with an embarrassed laugh. 'Not the politest thing to do, but I couldn't find the door and I thought it might be round here.'

I said nothing, having always thought that our front door was in a perfectly obvious place and wondering what sort of person might have difficulty in finding it. I was still in a slightly dazed state, after the shock of seeing his face at the window, but I pulled myself together and invited him to stay to lunch, calculating that there should be enough for one extra.

Alan had meantime given Rollo a drink and there was some feeble talk about the weather—it was indeed a beautiful day for late October—and Rollo said some gracious words about the charm of our provincial university town. He had not realised before how attractively set out were the Georgian buildings on the various levels of hills—and had it not been a watering place in the eighteenth century?

'Yes, indeed,' said Alan. 'There is still the old pump room.'

'Ah,' said Rollo and there was another silence. 'I wonder, does your wife know . . . ?' he said tentatively, with an equally doubtful glance at me. 'This business of that paper of yours . . .'

'Caro knows all that there is to be known,' said Alan accurately but rather pompously. 'You may speak quite freely.'

I felt a glow of pleasure, almost as if I had typed the paper or compiled its bibliography.

'Well, it's this. You know that Crispin wants to write a paper challenging yours—well, he's sent me a first draft. In it he implies that you have based your hypotheses on data that are either non-existent or that could not have been available to you had they existed.'

'Such a funny word, *data*.' I rushed into the conversation. 'I always imagine them as little dark things, aggressively plural and woe betide anyone who forgets it, like nails or cloves. Isn't it better to say "material"? Material sounds like an amorphous thing—homespun woollen or folk weave rather than exquisite brocade or silk . . .'

'Thank you, darling,' said Alan ironically as Rollo gave me a startled glance. 'But what are we going to do about Crispin? One can't allow oneself to be attacked in that way.'

'No, that's rather what I feel,' said Rollo. Perhaps with his two wives he had experienced enough strife and quarrels and regarded the journal as a place of rest, a nice scholarly refuge whose contributors would be above all envy and malice.

'Still,' Rollo went on, 'I did give him a chance to read it in manuscript—and you did, too, didn't you, Alan?'

'Yes. He said he was too busy. Now what on earth could *he* be too busy with?'

Both men smiled in a pitying way.

'Of course, he does have that great dog to exercise,' Alan was saying when the front door bell rang and Iris and Ian arrived, making it necessary for me to go into the kitchen to make the last-minute preparations.

When I appeared again to announce that lunch was ready and to try to force them into the dining room before the soup got cold, I could sense that there had been a change in the atmosphere. Alan and Ian were sitting silently, the latter rather like a sulky girl with his brooding expression and shoulder-length hair, while Iris and Rollo, evidently absorbed in each other's company, were carrying on the kind of conversation that is difficult to extend beyond the parties involved. It seemed that she had offered him an article for publication in the journal, or perhaps he had asked for one, for she was putting on a little-girl act, saying that she couldn't possibly write anything good enough to please *him*, but that it had always been her ambition, etc., etc., while Rollo looked fatuously pleased and pink in the face. He is a man easily flattered by women, I thought, and wondered if there was any advantage for us in this piece of knowledge.

I tried to be charming to Ian but found him not very responsive. He was obviously annoyed at the way Iris was making up to Rollo, but when Alan had poured some wine and managed to insinuate himself into their conversation, Ian and I were forced to do the best we could with each other. Tentatively I raised my glass.

'We ought to drink to something,' I suggested.

'Why?' he asked.

'Well, people do,' I said feebly, then, irritated by his lack of courtesy and what I took to be his left-wing condescension, I went on. 'Let's drink to your revolution—or whatever it is you people want!'

The moment I made the remark I regretted it but Ian smiled and touched his glass against mine. I suppose he thought I was just being silly.

'Tell me about Coco Jeffreys,' he said. 'I hear he's a friend of yours.'

'Coco Jeffreys?' I repeated, to gain time. 'What do you want to know about him?'

It was obvious that Ian wasn't at all interested in Coco as a person. He wanted to know about his work— his field research—where had that been? What had he published and where?

'He works down in the old part of town among the bus drivers and factory workers,' I explained.

'He studies racial tensions, I suppose,' Ian commented.

I wasn't sure about this and felt uncomfortable and inadequate.

'He gives out questionnaires for them to fill in, but I don't know yet what the results have been.'

'Are they at all organised down there?' Ian asked. 'Presumably they hang together as a community?'

'Yes, I think they do.'

'I haven't seen many of them up here in this part of the town,' said Ian reproachfully, as if it were my fault.

'Coco got one of them to dig his garden last year, and some of the women do domestic work.'

'And you think that's enough! To bring one or two of them out of their ghetto to work for you?'

'They do their own thing and we do ours,' I said coldly. 'What else would you suggest? Alan—I think people might like some more meat.'

At least Ian Ashton could eat, that was something. He was silent while he consumed a second helping and Iris, having caught the tail-end of our conversation and naturally wanting to join in where Ian was, started to enlarge upon the position of the Caribbeans in the town and whether one ought not to try to *do* something for them.

'Coco and his mother have tried, but the results were not altogether successful.'

'Can you wonder!' said Iris, her face flushed with drink and indignation, perhaps even love. 'That patronising kind of attitude may have been all very well on that island but it doesn't go down all that well here!'

The meal ended and we had coffee after which, greatly to my relief, Ian and Iris got up to go. Apparently they were going for a walk and had all the energy of people newly in love. I imagined them striding along criticising us and perhaps the meal, too, and then lying down and rolling about in the bracken.

Rollo Gaunt was in no hurry to leave. He insisted, in the aggressive way some guests do, that we should 'tackle' the washing up, so we were forced into the kitchen and began to talk again about the problems raised by the publication of Alan's article.

'Crispin mentioned a paper by a missionary called Stillingfleet. I believe you cited it as the crux of your argument. Where is it now?'

'Yes,' said Alan smoothly. 'I was able to consult it. The paper is now with the Stillingfleet Collection in our university library.'

'And accessible to scholars?' asked Rollo.

'Oh, yes,' said Alan. 'Perfectly accessible.'

The word seemed to please them both and they

considered it for a moment in silence. 'And it's now in the archives of the university library?' asked Rollo.

'I wouldn't exactly call them *archives*,' I put in. 'It's just an untidy old cupboard in the librarian's office.'

'Rollo was speaking metaphorically.' Alan frowned at my interruption.

'Well,' said Rollo briskly, 'I'm due at the Maynards' at four o'clock.'

'Oh, you're going there, are you?' said Alan casually.

'Yes, I suppose I ought to be on my way.'

We walked out with him to his car, his manner now seeming less intimate, as if he were preparing himself to meet the other side as it were. I wondered what he was going to say to Crispin about us. At least we had given him a good lunch. Perhaps that would count for something.

'If only we could follow him in there,' I said to Alan. 'What sort of terms is he on with Crispin?'

'An editor must be all things to all men.'

'That seems to give him and his world an exaggerated importance,' I protested, but then I considered that for some people, and that included us, it *was* of great importance. In the academic world what you published and where was about the most important thing there was.

'I wonder if he will publish Crispin's article,' said Alan. 'It could be out in March if he does.'

XXII

It was nearly two weeks before Dr. Cranton was back in the library. What at first had appeared to be just a cold had necessitated confinement to bed, then the getting up and finding his feet, then tottering out into the garden for a breath of fresh air, well wrapped up, then the first day back at work, tetchy and finding fault, and the going home early to be irritable to his little Mrs. Tiggy-Winkle wife who had tended him so lovingly throughout his illness and prepared dishes to tempt his capricious appetite.

On his second day back Dr. Cranton called me and Heather into his office. We had heard, he was sure, of Professor Maynard's impending retirement.

'Yes, we have heard,' we agreed.

'A great deal of fuss is being made about what is a perfectly natural event. Retirement is as natural as child-birth,' he declared, surprisingly I thought, for the two processes seemed to have little in common. I wondered if he had mentioned childbirth to embarrass us or to make us feel at home, since we were both mothers and had three children between us.

'The powers that be have decided that it would be a fitting gesture for the university library to organise an exhibition of manuscript Africana and other ethno-historical material in honour of work done by Professor Maynard in these fields,' Dr. Cranton went on. 'So you can imagine what that means—extra work for *us*! Now, you ladies, here is something that you can make your own. I want these papers sorted into neat bundles and the bundles done up in rubber bands and neatly labelled.'

I nearly asked how we should know what to label them. Then I realised that Dr. Cranton was giving us this opportunity of showing that our university education had not been wasted and flattering us by assuming that we were intelligent enough not to need further guidance.

'Now, if you would be good enough to start on these . . .' He pointed to two tea chests filled with papers which I did not remember having seen before.

'These were left to us under the will of the late Colonel Beddoes, who spent a good deal of his time in the Colonial Service in the Caribbean. They have been stored away in the basement since his death some twenty years ago—nobody having had the time to go through them before—and I have had them brought up to see the light of day, as it were.'

I remembered then that the tea chests had been brought up by the two West Indian porters who did odd jobs about the library. The chests had been the cause of a certain amount of grumbling since they were both heavy and unwieldy. I had wondered at the time what could be in them. I had certainly not imagined having to do anything with them myself.

'Is there anything else for the exhibition?' I asked.

'The Stillingfleet Collection. A recent acquisition which I shall deal with myself,' said Dr. Cranton.

'It won't be very exciting to *look* at,' I said to Heather as we began to pick gingerly about among the papers stuffed into the tea chests. 'Not exactly what one would call an *exhibition*—I suppose Professor Maynard will just come and glance through them.'

We worked on rather hopelessly, deterred by the damp, musty smell. Certainly the contents did not seem too difficult to arrange and classify, but of what value were they when this was done, I found myself asking. Unscientific 'Observations on the Native Inhabitants', lists of flora and fauna, the beginnings of a travel book of the old-fashioned kind, wallets of faded photographs—I could not see Crispin being interested in any of this stuff. Perhaps Coco might be, but it did not deal with his island. All the same, I mentioned it to him when we were having a drink together in the early evening.

'Poor Caro, what things you do get caught up in,' he teased, 'and all for the sake of fulfilling yourself and not wasting your higher education. Wasn't it better when you were reading to that old man in the old people's home?'

'I don't know—perhaps it was. That seemed more a work of charity and I wasn't paid for it.'

'Mother used to do such wonderful things on the island,' said Coco reminiscently. 'Works of charity and

of mercy. Just to see her did those poor women good—
they would crowd around her and finger her dresses.'

'The old people at Normanhurst didn't do that,' I
said. 'Anyway this stuff in the library is supposed to be
interesting and valuable. And somebody has to sort it
out.'

'All right, don't sound so militant,' said Coco.
'Maybe I'll come and have a look at it myself one of
these days.'

'You sound as if you thought it was a waste of
time, my working in the library,' I said, disgruntled.

'Well, practically all work's a waste of time, isn't
it? Especially for women. Why can't you just be beautiful and decorative and have lots of lovers?' he said idly.

'Oh, you're so silly,' I burst out. 'I'm neither beautiful nor decorative and even if I were who is there here
to be my lover?'

'Ian Ashton or that other young revolutionary?'
Coco suggested.

'Iris has snapped him up. I don't get a chance.'

I felt impatient and irritable with Coco, although
our conversation had not been serious. I suppose it was
the mention of Iris, of whom I was still a little jealous.
I could only console myself by speculating how long it
would be before Ian tired of her, and that was so un-
worthy of me that I was ashamed of finding consolation
in it. Looking forward to Crispin's presentation was
more congenial.

'Caro, have you decided yet what you are going to
wear?' Coco asked, his voice now quite animated. 'Mother
is having a new dress made—after all, it is something
of an occasion.'

'Oh yes, everybody will be there. I suppose I ought
to get something new myself.'

'I'll come and help you choose a gown,' offered Coco eagerly. 'You won't get it here, will you? Alan doesn't insist on choosing your clothes, does he?'

'I should hope not! I choose my own.'

'Yes,' said Coco doubtfully. 'I thought you probably did.'

XXIII

Strictly speaking, Crispin had retired at the end of the summer term but had wished to defer the presentation ceremony until the autumn because it seemed more appropriate for one who was, as he put it, in the autumn of life. Also, although this was not made public, the portrait had not been finished and the high point of the ceremony was to be its unveiling.

For the first few weeks of term, therefore, he had been hanging about the department, ostentatiously trying not to interfere, speaking of himself in a self-deprecating, half-joking way as 'an old buffer who used to work here', which was more embarrassing to his successor than if he had clung more obviously to his former position. Margaret told me she had tried to keep him at home when he would normally have been going to the university, but he was like an old actor, impatient and restless at the time when the curtain was due to go up, and it was very difficult to stop him from setting out, especially just before the Wednesday Seminar. In the end he had been invited to participate. They hadn't imagined he would really *want* to go on attending— good heavens, the younger ones thought, one would have given anything *not* to have gone. It would be another twenty years or so before they thought otherwise.

Eventually it was decided that the presentation should take place on the first of November in the Sophia Jennings Memorial Hall. First of all, Alan told me, the ceremony had been fixed for November the fifth, until somebody, worldly and practical, had pointed out that this was Guy Fawkes night, an occasion when the students might well indulge in youthful pranks, perhaps even a mild sort of riot. It was felt that this sort of danger should be avoided if at all possible. The fact that November the first was All Saints' Day did not pass without comment, but nobody was prepared to commit himself as to whether this date was appropriate or not. The only question that arose was whether the hall might be wanted for some religious purpose, though everyone was vague as to what that purpose might be.

The presentation was to be made by the Vice-Chancellor who, by a curious anomaly, happened to be one of Crispin's old students. This strange circumstance provided an obvious talking point both for the people assembled in the hall and those who were to make the speeches.

Coco and Kitty maintained their usual interest in who had been invited and what they were wearing.

'*Everybody* seems to be here,' said Kitty pettishly. 'I should have thought an occasion like this would be confined to university people.'

'Crispin was quite a figure in the town,' I pointed out, 'and he was very popular.'

'Why do middle-aged English women wear pastel colours,' Coco observed, 'when they so rarely suit them? Have they nobody to advise them?'

'Sometimes only the shop assistant anxious to make a sale,' I said.

'Caro, don't make things sound so sad—life is bad enough without that. A woman should always take along a friend to advise her. And don't tell me that some might not have a friend.'

I had spent a day in London and my sister had helped me to choose my new dress so Coco felt cheated, though he had grudgingly admitted that my dark red maxi-skirted dress suited me well enough.

'I almost prefer the women who haven't made any effort at all, but have just taken out an old evening dress of the fifties or even earlier. There's a sort of faded provincial grandeur about all that taffeta and lace and those "coatees".' He smiled at the word.

'Dresses were much prettier in those days,' Kitty lamented. 'But I never thought green suited Dolly— goodness knows how old *her* dress is.'

None of us could hazard a guess, but I was sure that I had seen the black velvet bridge coat she wore over it among some of her 'good' jumble. It may even have come from the dead wife of one of Dolly's old lovers.

Sister Dew, all in pink, came up to me. 'Poor old Reverend Stillingfleet,' she said, 'what a pity he couldn't be here today—he thought such a lot of Professor Maynard. Remember that lovely wreath the Professor sent to his funeral?'

I had to murmur something in agreement, for what she said was undeniably true. The old man would have enjoyed the occasion and he had thought a lot of Professor Maynard. It occurred to me that he would have preferred Crispin to use his unpublished material rather than Alan. Certainly he had refused to let Crispin see the manuscript when he asked, but perhaps that was only a kind of academic coyness. In the end, if Crispin had persevered he might have got what he wanted. What would Mr. Stillingfleet have really wished? Well, it was an academic question now.

'We've got another one now.' Sister Dew had lowered her voice to a confidential tone and had made the motion of drawing me away from Kitty and Coco.

'Another what?' I asked stupidly.

'Another old person with a box full of papers. It's funny what the old dears hang on to. Old love letters and that—I suppose they like to remember that somebody once wanted them, though you'd never think it now.'

'What sort of things are they?' I asked, out of habit.

'Oh, I don't know, dear. *I'm* not allowed to look. She's as bad as the Reverend Stillingfleet—won't let anyone open that box.'

'It's a woman, then?'

'A lady,' Sister Dew corrected me. 'Oh, look, there's Mrs. Cranton. You know she's knitting for Normanhurst.'

It was an inspiring slogan, the sort of thing that Menna Cranton, dogged little person that she was, would carry out nobly. Sister Dew moved over in her direction and I found myself facing Dr. Cranton.

There was a kind of glint in his eye and my thoughts went back to that strange moment at the Dabbs Memorial Lecture dinner. But the glint was sardonic and he was only inviting me to speculate on the kind of speeches we might expect when the portrait was unveiled—friends, Romans, countrymen—burying or praising, did I think? There could, of course, be alternatives. Yet this in itself was a sign of greater intimacy between us, unless, again, it was only the drink—for me one glass of sherry, for him two.

'A pity the exhibition at the library isn't actually ready at this moment,' I ventured. 'Then we might all have gone on there to look at it.'

'That kind of exhibition isn't meant to be *looked* at in the sense you imply,' he said testily. 'It is *mounted* as a tribute to the person concerned—simply that.'

'Still, it might have been—perhaps if we'd all worked overtime . . .' but he had turned away from me and now I could see that the unveiling ceremony was about to begin.

The Vice-Chancellor, Crispin's former pupil, made a good deal of this fact, bringing in Wordsworth's line about the child being father to the man and in this way transferring Crispin to a craggy Lakeland setting, wilder and ruggeder than our gentle hills where he walked with Prince, yet not unsuitable for the tall, noble-looking figure who now stood, half concealed yet expectant, at the side of the dais where the portrait, hidden by a grey velvet curtain, had been placed.

'Lovely *vel*vet,' Menna Cranton whispered. 'I wonder what they do with it after?'

'We shall know in a moment,' the Vice-Chancellor was saying, indicating the still shrouded portrait, 'how a distinguished contemporary artist has seen Crispin

Reginald Maynard, Professor Emeritus in this university. We may ask ourselves whether this is how *we* see Crispin, or whether it is how he sees himself.'

Crispin inclined his head and smiled at these last words.

'Or how he *thinks* he sees himself,' the Vice-Chancellor went on, almost inviting laughter.

He was obviously preparing us for what we were about to see so I guessed that the portrait must be in some way controversial.

I suppose an unveiling must always be greeted by a gasp of some kind and perhaps the best to be expected of 'a distinguished contemporary artist' is the usual number of eyes and other features and some faint likeness to the subject. I hoped that the portrait would at least be recognisable as the Crispin we knew or thought we knew, but when the curtain fell away from the painting there were exclamations, then an uneasy silence, broken only just soon enough by Margaret's strong voice, loyal both to the artist and to her husband, declaring vigorously, 'What a *splendid* piece of work! Isn't it Crispin to the life!' She was surrounded by her sons and daughters and their wives and husbands, and these now followed her lead by setting up a protective buzz of approval in which rather unlikely phrases could be picked out: 'most distinguished', 'fortunate indeed', 'a *speaking* likeness'.

'It isn't finished, is it?' Menna whispered.

'I *think* so,' I answered, but I could see what she meant for the portrait was of that school which prefers to leave a good deal to the viewer's imagination. To me it was disturbing, not so much because of the shadowy legs and the arms seeming to melt away without hands, as for the anguished expression of the face. It didn't look much like Crispin and yet I had the feeling that the artist had caught and displayed something one would rather not have seen, the vulnerable side that all human beings have, the inner doubts, the cry for help—things one didn't associate with Crispin at all. I felt myself in need of reassurance and put out my hand instinctively to touch a man's arm, thinking it would be Alan or even Coco, but it was Dr. Cranton. I withdrew my hand quickly, hoping he hadn't noticed. His comment—'Remarkable!', in his most sarcastic tone—suggested that he had not.

Then Iris came along. 'I think it's *super!*' she said in a bright, cocktail party voice, and things became ordinary again. People crowded round Crispin and the portrait and the tension was eased. Glasses were refilled and as I looked at the painting again I saw that I had been stupidly over-imaginative to read anything disturbing into it. It was quite a good portrait in a fashionable mid-twentieth-century style—there was no anguish, no cry for help, except, perhaps, in the eye of the beholder.

I went up to Crispin and added my congratulations, then tried to melt away, hoping that Alan would be ready to take me out to dinner. Rather to my surprise he was and seemed almost glad to leave the party.

'I feel Crispin has become too much of an embarrassment,' he explained. 'And now to make matters worse we shall have that dreadful painting looking down on us.'

'At least it won't follow you around the room with its eyes,' I said, 'as some portraits are said to do.'

'No, but we will be very conscious of it, at first anyway—then I suppose it'll just melt into the background.'

'I didn't realise it was going to hang in the department. I thought it had been presented to Crispin.'

'Ah, yes, so it had, but with low cunning he's given it back to us—can you beat *that*?'

I agreed, but it seemed fitting that Crispin should be allowed at least this triumph. As we sat at dinner in a rather embarrassingly *intime* little restaurant that had recently opened, I confided to Alan the news of the lady at Normanhurst with the box of papers. Might there be something there? I asked frivolously.

'Hush, Caro,' he said, frowning. Looking over his shoulder I could see at the next table Iris dining with Ian Ashton, and beyond them other university couples were revealed in the flickering light of the candles.

XXIV

The unveiling of Crispin's portrait marked the start of a round of university gaieties. One party led to another and we seemed to be going out every evening.

'Madame going out *again*,' said Inge reproachfully as I came downstairs on the evening of November the fifth.

'Oh, just to dinner,' I said quickly, as if that somehow made it better since eating could be regarded as a necessity rather than a frivolity. Anyway I had no reason to feel guilty where Inge was concerned for she was having the evening off to go to a fireworks party. Alan had dutifully lit a few sparklers for Kate after tea—there had been some talk of asking Luke and Alice but it had come to nothing. Luke was frightened of fireworks and

I had thought that the whole business might be forgotten but at the last minute Kate had demanded her rights. Now Alan and I were dining with Kitty and Coco, and Dolly was coming in to babysit.

She took her duties very seriously. Her battered canvas bag contained a selection of Victorian children's books from her shop, in case Kate awoke and needed entertaining, and she took care to write down in two places the telephone number of the hotel where we were having dinner 'in case of trouble'. We left her sitting broodily in front of the television which she would not admit that she wanted to watch. Alan had switched on BBC2 for the news and the evening's viewing included an old film of the thirties and a discussion about pollution, both of which should keep her interested. She would hardly be capable of switching over to the other channels, we imagined.

'Do you think she'll be all right?' Alan asked doubtfully.

'Of course—Inge has settled Kate and with any luck she shouldn't wake up.'

The hotel where Kitty and Coco had invited us to dine was a pleasant Georgian building in the square which was the centre of the older part of the town. As we left the car park Alan cast a backward look at the car and said, 'I hope they're not going to let off fireworks round here.' He seemed as anxious about the car as he had been about Kate.

'Don't worry,' I said. 'Let's relax and enjoy the evening.'

'That won't be easy,' he said gloomily, 'listening to poor Kitty recalling her salad days and Coco being silly with you.'

'Oh, there'll be lots of other things to talk about,' I said cheerfully, but the evening started so much like other evenings with Kitty and Coco that I began to wonder if I had been too optimistic. First of all I complimented Kitty on her dress (black lace with the famous black pearls) and that led to other occasions when she had worn it and the way they had of celebrating various festivals in the islands.

We had a table in the window and the curtains had not been drawn, which gave us a good view of anything that was happening in the square.

'I do hope some of the Caribbeans will come up here tonight,' she said. 'They do so love celebrations, especially fireworks.'

Alan sighed. 'I suppose it would do something towards integration,' he said to Coco, trying to raise the level of the conversation. 'They seem to live in such self-contained enclaves. I think you said you were working on a paper about this . . .' He paused, obviously trying to imagine the title of such an article. ' "Some Aspects of Segregation in a Caribbean Immigrant Community"?' he suggested.

'I hadn't got around to thinking of a title, but "Some Aspects" of something always sounds right, doesn't it?'

Alan looked rather annoyed. One did not joke about the titles of articles in learned journals, as I knew to my cost.

Kitty was beginning to look bored so I tried to distract her attention by pointing out Iris Horniblow, who was sitting in the opposite corner of the room with a rather meagre-looking man in a navy suit.

'That's the dress she wore when she gave the lecture,' I explained.

'Purple, is it?' said Kitty, not much interested. 'I can't wear that colour.'

'I think one calls it aubergine. I wonder who she's with?'

'Oh, that's her husband—Mr. Horniblow,' said Coco.

There was a surprised silence and I remembered what Alan had told me—that Iris had had a tough time, which somehow implied a rather different type of man from the one she was now having dinner with.

'Poor Mr. Horniblow,' said Coco. 'I suppose she has no further use for him now.'

Alan looked as if he were about to protest but then said mildly enough, 'I always thought *he* had left *her.*'

'Oh, no doubt Iris gave that impression, but it was the other way round. *She* left *him* and took the children with her.'

'She was driven to it, perhaps?' I suggested, not without malice.

'By boredom, maybe,' Coco agreed. 'She used his influence to get a research grant and on the strength of that she got her job here.'

'How do you know so much about it all of a sudden?' I asked.

'Oh, one hears things,' Coco said vaguely.

'I wonder why they're having dinner together now then.'

'It's a civilised thing to do,' Alan broke in, apparently determined to say something in Iris's favour. 'Surely that's why.'

'I expect she wants more money from him,' said Coco simply. 'Or he may have been to see the children.'

'I can never understand a woman having to ask a

man for money,' said Kitty. 'It seems quite unnatural to me.'

'Shall we have our coffee here?' Coco suggested. 'There seems to be something going on in the square and we shall get a good view.'

I noticed with relief that Iris and her companion had gone and she need no longer monopolise the conversation.

'It doesn't seem very exciting,' said Kitty. 'If only those girls could see how terrible they look.'

Kitty could not get used to the sight of the girl students with untidy flowing hair in long bedraggled skirts, and it was useless to point out that this happened to be the current fashion. I recognised one of the girls in the square as the one who had borrowed my sewing machine and wondered what she was up to now. As far as I could see she seemed to be filling a large wheeled shopping basket with what I used to call 'kiddy-food'— sliced loaves of white bread, packets of fish fingers, sausages, baked beans and Coca-Cola.

'Surely they haven't been shopping *now*?' I said. 'All the shops will have shut hours ago. What can they be doing?'

'Will you have a liqueur, Caro?' Coco asked.

'Thank you, yes,' I said absently, for coffee and liqueurs seemed far from the scene I was observing, where now another girl came along with more sliced loaves and a large enamel teapot.

'It looks like a kind of Guy Fawkes night feast,' said Alan indulgently. 'And the girls are getting the food together, very properly.'

'They'll be making a bonfire somewhere?' asked Kitty. 'Can we see that?'

A crowd of young men and women was now filling the square and forming into a rather straggly procession, headed by an effigy of the current Prime Minister. It all seemed quite harmless and suitable—a protest march on a fine evening and food eaten round a bonfire. Our students' demonstrations were usually very mild affairs—a few banners being waved and shouts that someone or other must 'go'.

The procession moved off and we sat peacefully drinking our coffee and liqueurs and speculating on where the students were going to make their protest. In the distance we heard the sound of chanting and of fireworks being let off, and there were bursts of stars as rockets soared into the night sky. After a while a police car went by, its siren blaring and then, more disturbingly, a fire engine.

As we left the hotel and came out into the car park it became obvious from the noise and the excitement that something was happening around the university buildings.

'I think we should go up there,' I said and Alan reluctantly agreed, though I could see that he did not like taking the car into what he considered to be a potentially dangerous situation.

As we drove up to the university buildings I noticed a crowd round the sculpture, the one that resembled a pair of outspread thighs. One of the girls had begun to unload her basket and proceeded to use the sculpture as a table, spreading the sliced loaves with margarine and some kind of potted meat.

'A use for that at last!' said Coco, pointing it out. 'I often wondered what it was for.'

Now we could smell smoke and as we rounded the

corner and came to the library we found the fire engines with a tangle of hoses and confusion everywhere.

'It is very terrible,' Kitty moaned. 'I don't think I can bear it.'

'I think we ought to go and tell Evan Cranton,' I said, feeling that as a worker in the library—even if only part-time—I should be doing something and this seemed the only thing I could do.

Alan was obviously anxious to leave the scene so he turned the car quickly and headed for the Crantons'.

Menna opened the door to us. She had presumably gone to bed early since she was wearing a pink fluffy wool dressing gown and a hairnet of the same colour.

'I've just made some tea,' she announced and showed us into the sitting room where a number of cups and saucers were set out on a table as if she was expecting a party.

Dr. Cranton, fully dressed, was sitting calmly in an armchair.

'Tea?' he enquired, 'or would you prefer something stronger?'

'Tea would be lovely,' I murmured, relieved that he did not appear more upset.

'So Rome is burning,' he said, when we were all served with tea.

Some of us smiled uneasily, aware of the implications behind his words. But what could we have done, what could we do now?

'The police were there,' said Alan, 'and the fire brigade.'

'Yes, they rang me, of course. And George Armitage is there. He can be a hero if he likes.'

'Will he be able to do anything?' I asked.

'No, but he will have made the gesture.'

We could all have made gestures, I thought, though perhaps Kitty would not have been expected to. I felt a little ashamed now that we had not.

'The unfortunate effect of student pyrotechnics, as you will have deduced,' Evan Cranton said. 'An ill-aimed rocket broke a window and started a fire—though I have no details as yet.'

I think we were all relieved when the telephone rang and he went out into the hall to answer it.

Menna busied herself refilling cups. 'Such a business. *Vandalism*, I call it!'

'Well, it is over.' Evan Cranton came back into the room. 'The police superintendent informs me that everything is under control. The books and the library itself are unharmed. By a strange coincidence'—here his voice took on its customary ironic tone—'my office alone suffered damage, so that only *I* will be inconvenienced. You will be interested to hear that what was a minor conflagration has been elevated to the level of a major inconvenience by the excess zeal of our noble fire service. In their enthusiasm they saturated the room with water thereby destroying all the papers and manuscripts, reducing them to an illegible pulp.'

'Colonel Beddoes' papers!' I exclaimed. 'All the work Heather and I did—all for nothing!'

Dr. Cranton inclined his head.

'And'—a dreadful thought struck me—'the Stillingfleet Collection!'

'The Stillingfleet Collection,' Dr. Cranton repeated sarcastically. 'How fine it sounds, doesn't it, when it's given a name? I suppose that is how we will think of it in future, the Stillingfleet Collection.'

'That was the old man at Normanhurst, wasn't it?'

said Menna chattily. 'The one that had a box of papers.'

'A box of papers. Perhaps my wife has supplied the true estimate. After all, what were they?'

Alan opened his mouth as if to speak but I, seizing the excuse of Kitty's tiredness, said we must be on our way, and the question was left without an answer. Certainly the Stillingfleet papers were no longer accessible to scholars.

XXV

The destruction of the man-
uscript Africana and other documents did not make
headline news, even in the local paper. There were a
couple of paragraphs on an inside page and a brief but
thoughtful editorial on student indiscipline and the more
general danger of fireworks, but since the damage was
relatively slight no one paid much attention to it.

Only Crispin and Margaret Maynard showed any
concern, Crispin, because now he would not be able to
consult the Stillingfleet papers to see just what Alan's
sources had been for his article, and Margaret for a more
prosaic reason. She saw that the work for Evan Cranton's retirement—the great Bibliography—had been de-

stroyed and she felt sorry for Menna who would have
to bear the brunt of his disappointment.

I decided to ask Crispin and Margaret to dinner,
especially now that his article 'attacking' Alan was to be
published. It seemed best to make a bold gesture and
we owed them so much hospitality. I wondered if the
subject would be mentioned over dinner but in the event
we talked mostly of their moving to a smaller house in
a village some distance away and the difficulties involved.

'Of course, we shall spend a lot of time in Italy,'
said Margaret in an encouraging tone as she glanced
towards Crispin.

I could see that life in Italy would be easier for her.
She would be able to relax and not have to keep him
away from the university.

'You'll be able to write your book now,' I said to
Crispin, and evidently it was the right thing to say for
he became quite genial and at the end of the evening,
just as he and Margaret were leaving, he drew Alan aside
and said something to him in a confidential tone, something that was to be a secret from Margaret and me.

'What was that?' I asked as the front door closed.

'Oh, nothing really.' Alan seemed unwilling to
tell me.

'Some ethnological shop?' I persisted.

'Not that, exactly. Oh, I suppose you'd better know.
He thinks *you* had something to do with getting hold
of that manuscript and said how lucky I was to have a
wife who would do that for me.'

'I see.' Well, it was only to be expected. I, as a
woman, could take the blame and all my efforts to help
Alan would be nothing beside this one unscholarly and

deceitful thing which Crispin could not bring himself to believe that Alan could really have done himself.

This gesture of reconciliation on Crispin's part seemed, somehow, to open the way for Alan's advancement—Senior Lecturer, Reader, Professor even—there would be no stopping him now. I saw us moving on to other universities, perhaps even to America. Life suddenly seemed more full of possibilities.

'Do you want to go on working in the library?' Alan asked me. 'You *could* go and help Dolly in her shop if you'd rather.'

I remembered what he had once thought about this and was amused at the kind of reward he seemed to be offering me.

'No, I think I'll go on working in the library,' I said firmly.

'Well, now that all that manuscript material has been destroyed . . .' Alan began.

'I suppose you could say that all the work Heather and I were doing was in vain.'

'In a sense, yes.'

'But can't it have its own reward? The peculiar satisfaction of a symphony that has never been performed or a painting seen only by the artist?'

'Or an article never published?' Alan added. 'There's not much satisfaction *there*.'

'I think Evan Cranton would want me to go on,' I said. 'After all, I can do other things like sticking labels on the backs of books and typing out cards.'

'*I* might occasionally have some typing for you,' said Alan graciously.

'Thank you, darling.'

'Will you go on reading at Normanhurst?'

'I suppose I may as well—at least it's useful work.'

'More useful than helping me?'

The question hung in the air, unanswered.

Of course I did go to Normanhurst, out of curiosity as much as anything else. It was now winter and no old people were to be seen walking carefully on the grass or the gravel paths. Only the evergreen bushes remained as I had seen them on that first day, and Sister Dew's bright welcoming smile.

'Well, Mrs. Grimstone dear, this *is* a nice surprise!' Perhaps the welcoming smile was even brighter than I had remembered. 'Come to read to my old people, have you? That *is* kind. And we've got Mrs. Armitage here now. She comes two evenings a week—such a help.'

'Heather?' I said in astonishment.

'Is that what they call her? Such a pretty name, Heather, don't you think so?'

'Who is she reading to?' I asked.

'An old gentleman who's just come in—and, would you believe it, *he's* got a box of papers just like poor old Reverend Stillingfleet!'

Not *exactly* like, I said to myself, or at least it was to be hoped not.

'Some book on mathematics he was writing,' Sister Dew went on, 'and he wants the papers to go to the library here when he passes on. Mrs. Cranton was thrilled when I told her!'

I wondered if Evan Cranton had been equally thrilled. If it got about among the old people that the library welcomed such bequests goodness only knew what it might end up with.

'She's been knitting bed-jackets for the old ladies,

Mrs. Cranton has. I must show you—they're really dainty.'

'So there's really nothing for me to do,' I said, as much to myself as to Sister Dew.

'Don't you believe it!' she said in her briskest nurse's voice. 'There's that lady I told you about.'

'Yes, so you did. Does she want somebody to read to her?'

'Oh, yes, she's a *great* one for books. I'll take you to see her.'

Miss Veitch was sitting up in bed wearing one of Menna Cranton's bed-jackets, mauve, with matching ribbons. She was frail-looking with soft white hair standing out from her bony head in a kind of halo or nimbus. When Sister Dew introduced us and said that I was going to read to her, Miss Veitch clasped her hands and exclaimed in a faint voice, 'Oh, how kind! I find reading difficult now and I do so love a good book!'

Well, at least I wouldn't be reading anthropological or sociological works to her, I thought. 'Good' books must mean the classics—Jane Austen, Dickens, George Eliot—things one had been meaning to re-read or even read for the first time. I hoped it wouldn't be Scott.

Sister Dew handed me the book I was to read from. It certainly wasn't Scott, nor was it Dickens, George Eliot or Jane Austen. The coloured picture on the jacket showed a handsome young man in surgeon's dress, presumably in an operating theatre. By his side was an exceptionally pretty young nurse who appeared to be handing him something.

'I've read that one,' Sister Dew whispered to me. 'He was Surgical Registrar on the way up, very promising and all that, when he made a mistake that nearly cost him his career. If it hadn't been for *her* . . . well, I expect you can guess the rest and I mustn't spoil *your* enjoyment.'

I opened the book and began to read. The story certainly held my attention until certain falsely romantic touches began to jar on me.

Miss Veitch lay back on her pillows, smiling contentedly.

'I like books about hospitals,' she said. 'I might have married a surgeon once.'

'Oh?' I was politely interested and wondered if I was going to get her whole life-story.

'But it was not to be,' she sighed. 'I've got all his letters in a box.'

'Goodness,' I exclaimed.

'Yes—and all the love letters I've ever had. All in that box. That must seem very foolish to you.'

'No, of course not.' I couldn't think what to say. Obviously people did keep their lives in boxes, or at least people of that generation. There was something gruesome and pathetic about it. I'd never kept any of Alan's letters or even David's. But then I suppose there hadn't been all that many. People didn't seem to write love letters nowadays.

'Hospital romances,' I said to Dolly that evening when she called round to see us. 'That's what I'm reading now. It's a far cry from Mr. Stillingfleet's stuff.'

'Maybe, but it is all *life*,' said Dolly in her firmest tone, 'and no aspect of life is to be despised.'

'I suppose it may do something for me—Coco would say that it might make me more loving and feminine. Do you think it might have that effect?'

'Is that what you want?' asked Dolly unhelpfully.

'I'm not sure that it's what *I* want,' said Alan, coming into the room with a bundle of typescript in his hand. 'I rather hoped Caro would retype this for me. It's my answer to Crispin's attack on me.'

'And will it be published?' I asked.

'Rollo has agreed to publish it,' said Alan, with an air of smugness.

'Then perhaps Crispin will attack again?'

'Crispin is an old man,' said Dolly. 'It may be too much for him.'

'I doubt that,' said Alan.

I thought how 'ongoing' life was and was at that moment glad of it. Later I might change my mind.

'I suppose the hedgehogs are all gone now?' I said to Dolly.

'Yes, we don't see them now, of course, they're in hibernation. But in April—oh, that will be the time!'